TITUS

LANTERN BEACH BLACKOUT: DANGER RISING, BOOK 4

CHRISTY BARRITT

CHAPTER
ONE

PRESLEY LENNOX'S heart pounded as she unlocked the door to her apartment.

As she twisted the key, she glanced behind her.

She was the only one in the hallway.

But she felt on edge.

She'd been on edge for the past two years—and that was on a good day.

On a bad day . . .

She shivered.

She couldn't think about that right now.

Her boyfriend, Alex, had a meeting tonight, which meant she had this evening to herself. The time alone was a welcome reprieve.

Presley stepped into her apartment and locked the door behind her.

For the past few months, she'd constantly felt as if

she was being watched. Had Alex hired someone to spy on her?

The man was controlling, to say the least. Every time she tried to call things off between them . . . she couldn't.

Whether he used manipulation or intimidation, Alex always found a way to make her stay.

Tears pressed at her eyes at the thought.

By all appearances, she was a free woman. However, she felt like a prisoner shackled by her life choices.

As she stood just inside the door, she drew in a deep breath, determined to pull herself together. She would enjoy this evening.

Watch some TV. Eat a good meal.

Dream about ways to escape.

She deposited her purse on a hook before stepping into her living room.

As she did, she froze.

Someone sat in the chair in the corner.

His features shadowed.

Imposing.

Dangerous.

Presley gasped, stumbling backward as alarms sounded in her head.

Would Alex carry through with his promise that if he couldn't have her, no one could? Did he sense she still wanted to leave? That she was planning how to do so?

Had he sent someone to kill her?

She grabbed the heavy candlestick from the table beside her and held it like a baseball bat.

She wouldn't go down without a fight.

"Presley . . . it's me." As soon as Titus Armstrong saw Presley's eyes widen with fear, he rose to his feet.

He hadn't intended on scaring her—he simply needed privacy. It was the only reason he hadn't approached Presley in a more conventional way.

"Who are you?" Her voice wavered as she stared into the shadows.

Titus stepped toward the dim light emanating from her aquarium so Presley could see his face. "It's me . . . Titus."

She sucked in a breath then lowered the candlestick to her side almost as if she'd gone weak. "Titus?"

"I'm sorry. I didn't mean to scare you, but I had to talk to you."

Titus stared at Presley, the woman who had broken his heart and brought him to his knees.

She looked just as beautiful as ever.

Presley was the kind of woman who turned heads wherever she went. She had straight blonde hair that came just below her shoulders, a slim build, naturally sun-kissed skin, and perfectly balanced features. Her blue eyes were striking, and her smile—when she offered it—could knock someone off their feet.

She looked much more tamed than she once had. Just two years ago, her hair had flowed down her back in long layers. Now it hung neatly trimmed. Back then, she'd barely worn any makeup. Now mascara accentuated her eyes, and a rosy lipstick graced her lips. When they'd first met, she'd loved nothing more than jean shorts and T-shirts. Now her clothes were neat and fitted.

Seeing her again only reminded Titus of how hard he had fallen for her.

And, instead, Presley had fallen hard for his half-brother.

Titus shoved aside those emotions, knowing they'd get him nowhere at the moment. They had far more important matters to discuss.

Presley raised the candlestick again, caution skimming her gaze. "What are you doing in my apartment?"

"I'm sorry to frighten you, but this was the only way I could talk with you without raising any alarms."

Her eyes narrowed with skepticism, and her fear remained. "What does that mean? Why are you back in Greensboro even?"

"I need to talk to you."

"So, you broke into my apartment?"

"It's important, and it's best if we do this alone."

"How did you know I would be here alone tonight? Have you been . . . have you been following me?" Her voice sounded breathless with realization and fear.

Titus pressed his lips together. This wasn't going how he envisioned. "It's not what it sounds like. I just had to be certain no one saw me with you."

"So, you *have* been watching me?" Presley stared at him with questions in her big blue eyes.

As much as Titus wanted to dislike Presley, right now he only wanted to reassure her. He hated the fear in her gaze.

"Can I just explain?" He kept his voice even and almost pleading, his shoulders relaxed, his motions easy.

She shook her head, still gripping that candlestick —a wooden one that would offer little protection in the face of real danger. Titus didn't tell her that, though.

"I don't know what there is to explain," she rushed. "In fact, maybe I should call the police."

He raised his hand, trying to control her alarm. "Please. I'm not here to hurt you. I'm not that kind of guy. You know that."

Presley stared at him, doubt in her gaze.

Doubt? What had Titus ever done to make her doubt what kind of man he was? He'd never so much as gotten angry around her when they'd been dating. Besides, she'd been the one who dumped him.

More tension twisted around his spine.

He had to get through to her. Time was of the essence here. It was the only reason he'd come.

"Presley . . . please." He tilted his head as his eyes implored hers. "I wouldn't be here unless it was important."

She stared at him another moment before finally nodding. "You have five minutes. Then I'm going to scream for help."

PRESLEY DIDN'T BOTHER to offer Titus anything to drink as they sat at the kitchen table.

As far as she was concerned, this wasn't a friendly visit.

And if Alex found out his brother was here . . . she shuddered to think about his reaction. Last she'd heard, Titus was still a SEAL. Still stationed in Virginia Beach.

Why had he come back to his hometown of Greensboro, North Carolina? Just to talk to her?

She stared across the table at Titus, the man she'd once been madly in love with. It had been two years since she'd seen him, and he looked better now than ever. But it was more than his looks that had caught her attention in the past. It was his character and tenderness and the way he'd believed in her.

Only she'd been so wrong when it came to love. . . she still wasn't sure how she'd allowed Alex to pull the wool over her eyes so easily.

Being with Titus . . . he'd brought down all her walls, and she'd been happy for the first time in her life. Then everything exploded and transformed her into a shell of the person she'd once been.

"Presley . . ." Titus leaned toward her, his elbows on the table. The position showed his bulging biceps, a reminder that he kept himself in shape. That he was a warrior. That he'd put his life on the line for his country uncountable times.

Not only that . . . but the piney scent of his cologne made her thoughts tumble back in time.

She swallowed, her throat dry, but she managed to croak out a "Yes?"

He still hesitated, almost as if he didn't want to tell her whatever he had to say. So why was he here? Why the cloak-and-dagger meeting?

"A lot has happened since we saw each other last." He glanced at the table, the motion showing his expressive eyes and long lashes—lashes entirely too thick for a man. "I got out of the military not long ago, and I'm now working with an organization called Blackout. It's a private security group based out of Lantern Beach, North Carolina."

"Okay . . ." She still had no idea where he was going with this.

"We've been investigating something that I believe you're connected with, and we need your help."

Presley blanched. That had been the last thing she'd expected to hear. His words caused the nerves at her spine to pinch. "What are you investigating? What could I possibly help with?"

Titus pressed his lips together, not bothering to hide his hesitation. He didn't want to have this conversation either, did he? In fact, he didn't even want to be here.

"Our investigation involves an organization called The System."

All the air left her lungs.

The System?

How did Titus know about that? The group was supposed to be top secret. Private.

As was her involvement with it.

Quickly, she scooted her chair back and swung her head back and forth.

Whatever he was about to ask her to do, Presley already knew the answer was an emphatic no.

This conversation already wasn't going as Titus had planned.

But somehow, he had to convince Presley to help him.

He'd told his superiors that anyone besides him would be better for this mission. But they'd insisted Titus was perfect.

So now, here he was facing his past in order to protect his future. He only wished he could skip this in-the-moment stuff.

His gaze locked with hers. "Can you at least hear me out?"

Presley stared at him another moment, her eyes narrowed with reservation. "Go ahead. You still have three minutes."

He shifted in his seat, praying he'd find the right words. "Presley . . . we know that you're involved with The System."

She raised her chin. "What do you mean . . . involved?"

"You know what I mean. We have drone footage showing you at the compound that was raided up in the mountains of North Carolina a few weeks ago."

Her eyes flickered with surprise before the emotion disappeared, but she offered nothing else. No denial. No confirmation.

Only a tense face and a deep swallow.

Titus reached into his pocket and pulled out a photo of her on the property. Blackout's drone had taken the picture, and Titus had been the one to identify her among the crowd gathered there.

Presley's eyes widened as she glanced at the image. There was no denying her affiliation now, even if she wanted to.

He stooped slightly as he tried to make eye contact. "Presley, we know this group is planning something big. Something dangerous. We need to stop them. But in order to do that, we need someone inside the group's inner circle."

"That's not possible. They don't let just *anyone* inside the core group." She pressed her lips together as if she hadn't meant to share that much.

When she didn't say anything else, he continued. "When millionaire Seymour Whitlock was dying, his last wish was that we—Blackout—get to the bottom of whatever it is The System is up to. That's what we're doing. But this is more than a job to us. It's an obligation out of love for our country."

She played with the edge of a rattan placemat in front of her, clearly nervous. Her gaze skittered all over the place as if her mind was trying to make sense of topsy-turvy thoughts.

"Alex got you involved, didn't he?" Titus studied her face, searching for the truth.

Presley went still as if she didn't want to answer—or as if she had just gotten caught.

She didn't respond.

She wasn't going to make this easy, was she?

"Presley, I don't know how much you know about what's going on. But I feel certain that Alex *does* know something. You're our chance of figuring out the truth."

"I don't know anything." Presley's voice cracked. "I'm just an accessory to Alex. He and the other guys keep me in the dark."

At least, Titus was getting *somewhere*. Presley had offered *something*.

"My colleagues and I believe these guys are planning a domestic terrorist attack. And, if that's true, the stakes here are bigger than you and me."

"A domestic terrorist attack?" Her lips parted in shock.

Titus observed her a moment. Her wide eyes showed earnest surprise.

Had Alex truly kept her out of the loop?

Titus swallowed hard. "That's what the intel we've been given indicates. But we need more details if we're going to stop these guys."

She shook her head as if trying to comprehend his words. "Even if that's true . . . I'm still not sure what you think I can do. Maybe you should talk to Alex."

Titus leaned closer, knowing it was time to close the deal. "I need an inside source. Presley, I'm only asking because I'm desperate."

Her gaze locked with his, fear swirling in the depths of her eyes. "You have no idea what you're asking me to do, Titus. You're asking me to put my life in danger."

PRESLEY'S MIND RACED.

Titus couldn't be serious.

Yet everything suddenly made sense.

He would come here only if he was desperate. And Titus was *clearly* desperate right now.

But a domestic terrorist attack? That couldn't be true.

Presley wanted to deny that could happen. She'd discovered staying below the radar was the best way to operate—if she wanted to stay alive.

But could she continue doing that knowing innocent people's lives were at risk?

Alex had only told her The System was planning some kind of event as their announcement to the world that they existed.

But what if they were planning something far more deadly than Alex had let on?

Her limbs trembled as she thought about the fallout from an incident like the one Titus mentioned.

She'd stuck her head in the sand for far too long.

But Titus' request . . . she couldn't do it.

She couldn't be an inside source. Alex would see right through her the moment she started asking questions.

Titus reached across the table for her hand. He seemed to think twice about it and drew his arm back toward him instead.

His gaze connected with hers. "You know I wouldn't be here unless it was important."

"If Alex finds out that you're in my apartment right now . . ." Presley could only imagine his reaction.

Most people didn't know about the controlling side of him. They knew him as a brilliant, well-respected lawyer.

But behind closed doors was a different story.

"I know I'm asking a lot. Promise me you'll think about it, at least?" Titus pleaded with her with his gaze.

"I don't know . . ." Her stomach roiled. If she got caught . . . She flinched as she imagined the pain she would endure.

"We don't have much time, Presley. The attack is supposed to happen in five days. It's something they are calling The Great Awakening."

Her breath caught. "What? Where? How?"

"We don't know. That's what we need to figure out—with your help."

"How do you even know any of this? It sounds like you already have an inside source."

He swallowed hard. "We had a contact who was willing to talk—but only on the phone. In the middle of him telling us more details, the line went dead. We found out the next morning he'd died of a supposed 'heart attack.'"

"Titus . . ." Her voice cracked as she shook her head.

This was all a nightmare, right? She would wake up at any time.

Only she knew she wouldn't.

This wasn't the position she wanted to be in. She'd become good at self-preservation.

Titus' request put that to the test.

"I can give you time to think this through and come back tomorrow," Titus said. "But time isn't a luxury right now—not with so much at risk."

As more alarm raced through her, Presley quickly shook her head, panicked at the thought of meeting with him again. "You can't come back tomorrow. Someone will see you."

He shook his head. "I'm good at what I do. No one will see me."

"Titus . . ."

"I'll protect you, Presley."

His words—spoken without so much as a hint of doubt—nearly brought tears to her eyes.

Protect her?

Titus had been so noble when they'd dated.

But then everything turned upside down, and Alex had swept in like Prince Charming.

Only he wasn't.

Not by a long shot.

She was a terrible judge of character—clearly. But she'd made her bed, and now she had to sleep in it, as the saying went.

Titus' phone buzzed. As he glanced down at it, his eyes widened.

Something was wrong. Presley was certain of it.

"Titus?" Her voice cracked.

He glanced up, alarm filling his gaze. "One of my guys just saw Alex . . . he's coming into your apartment building right now."

All the blood drained from Presley's face as she thought about the punishment she'd receive if Alex caught his brother in her apartment without his permission.

What was she going to do?

Titus watched as Presley's face paled.

Her expression left no room for doubt that she was scared—maybe even terrified.

He rose to his feet, desperate to make this situation right. "I'll explain that I stopped by looking for him."

Presley frantically shook her head. "No, that won't work. You've got to hide."

"Hide?"

She rushed to her feet, took his arm, and began tugging him toward the bedrooms. "If you leave now, he'll see you. He'll know. Did you leave anything behind to indicate that you were here?"

Titus' phone was in his pocket, and he hadn't touched anything else. "No."

She continued pulling him with surprising strength until she reached a closet in the primary bedroom and opened the door. "Stay in here, and don't make a sound. Promise me."

He studied her, unable to fight the confusion plaguing him.

Her reaction was so unexpected.

But he knew, based on the fear in her gaze, that he couldn't argue. "I'll stay in here. I won't make a sound. I promise."

She stared at him another moment, her eyes wide and her motions shaky. Finally, she shut the door and stepped back.

His mind continued to race. Titus knew Alex had a Type A personality. That he could even be a micro-manager.

But Presley's reaction . . . it indicated much more than that.

He tried not to jump to conclusions, but how could he not? She was clearly walking on eggshells right now.

Titus remained perfectly still, just as he'd promised.

Then he waited.

The scent of vanilla drifted from the clothes surrounding him. The scent tried to take his mind back in time. He resisted the urge to lean closer, to get a better whiff.

Too much was on the line right now to give in to that kind of indulgence.

Instead, when he heard Alex's voice, he braced himself for whatever would happen next.

CHAPTER
FOUR

PRESLEY QUICKLY GLANCED around her apartment and confirmed everything was in place. Then she straightened the blouse she wore, along with her skirt, and tossed her hair over her shoulder.

As she heard the knock at the door, she tried to compose her expression so Alex wouldn't grow suspicious.

With another deep breath, she opened the door and offered a wide, welcoming smile to her boyfriend.

The man was a knockout, that was for sure. The star of his college football team. Straight A student. Graduated at the top of his class from law school.

Not only was he athletic and smart, but he was handsome—six feet, two inches tall with broad shoulders, a square jaw, and light-brown hair that he kept short. His eyes were always assessing, his mind always working, his mannerisms always confident.

Yes, he turned heads everywhere he went. Yet in a different way than Titus.

Titus had always been understated, acting as if he didn't like the attention.

Alex *loved* adoration and valued being thought of highly.

"Alex . . . I wasn't expecting to see you tonight." Presley pushed a strand of her honey-blonde hair behind her ear. "I thought you said you had a meeting."

As he stepped closer and kissed her cheek, Presley tried not to flinch. His touch made her feel an equal mix of fear and disgust.

"It was cancelled," he told her. "So, I decided to stop by and see you. Can you make something to eat? I'm famished."

Something to eat? Presley's mind raced, though she tried not to show it.

That meant Alex would be here at least an hour.

And that, in turn, meant Titus would need to stay quiet in her closet that same length of time.

Her pulse thumped harder in her ears.

Whichever way she looked at it, Presley knew she couldn't tell Alex no—not if she knew what was best for her.

He didn't wait for her answer. Instead, he stepped farther inside, his presence instantly owning the place.

As it should.

He'd picked the apartment out for her as well as the furnishings. Every time Presley had suggested a couch or table, Alex reminded her that her sense of style was lacking.

It's not you, my love. It's your upbringing. You didn't grow up with the finer things. But I'll teach you. I'll make you into someone—the person I know you're capable of being.

Alex paused in the living room and sniffed.

Presley froze.

Could he smell Titus' cologne? His shampoo? Were Alex's senses that good?

She swallowed hard, but her saliva nearly choked her.

"Everything okay?" She tried to loosen her voice.

He kept his head raised, his shoulders tight. "Yes, there's just a peculiar smell in here. Almost piney."

Piney? That *could* be Titus' cologne.

Tension crept up her spine, but she tried to play it off. "Must be the new bathroom cleaner I bought."

He nodded as if her explanation satisfied him. "You're right. That must be it."

A whiff of air left her lungs—but it was too early

to feel relief.

First, she needed to figure out what to cook. She'd planned on Mexican. Something hot and spicy—two things Alex hated. If she wanted that type of food, she ate it only when she was alone.

Presley walked into the kitchen and opened the refrigerator door, her mind racing. She didn't want to pick the wrong type of food and set Alex off.

Once, after she'd fixed him beef stew and had forgotten to leave out the carrots, he'd gotten so angry that he'd thrown his whole bowl on her. Then he'd made her eat the rest of her own portion while he watched and glared.

She cleared her throat, again composing herself. "I could make spaghetti. How does that sound?"

She held her breath as she waited for his response.

A smile fluttered across his lips. "Sounds like the perfect comfort food after the day I've had."

Presley smiled back at him.

But she wasn't sure her nerves could handle the tension of this moment.

As Presley began chopping up an onion and cooking the ground beef, Alex stood behind her and slipped his arms around her waist.

Presley tried not to stiffen. Instead, she let out a soft giggle—a fake one, though she hoped Alex didn't sense that. "You seem like you're in a good mood considering you just said you had a bad day."

"I know I've been busy lately," he murmured in her ear. "I'm sorry I haven't had much time to spend with you."

His lack of attention had been a blessing. A relief. A wonderful reprieve.

All things she couldn't say.

"I understand," she said instead as she added some onion and garlic to the meat in the skillet. "It's really okay."

"We're still planning The Great Awakening, and it's taking up all my energy it seems."

The Great Awakening?

That was what Titus had mentioned. Why hadn't she heard about it before?

She nibbled the inside of her lip.

Was Titus making assumptions when he said The System was planning a domestic terrorist attack?

Presley had thought this upcoming event would be some type of advertising push.

But something that could destroy innocent people's lives?

Titus *had* to be mistaken.

Alex and his friends . . . they were dogmatic and determined. Maybe idealistic even.

But they wouldn't hurt innocent people . . . would they?

She swallowed hard.

How could she even ask herself that question?

Alex had hurt *her* on many occasions. Even if she *had* provoked him, she hadn't deserved the punishment she'd gotten in return.

Yes, he and his friends were definitely capable of inflicting pain on others.

Any doubt left her mind.

Alex slipped away from her and moved to the other side of the kitchen island instead.

Presley started boiling the water for the pasta as she glanced up at him. "So, what exactly are you planning for The Great Awakening?"

Alex stared at her, his eyes flickering with an unreadable emotion. "You'll see. I want it to be a surprise."

"Will I be involved?"

He grinned. "I hope so. You're going to want to be a part of the day that we make history."

Make history? That definitely sounded bigger than a promotional campaign.

"You can't even give me a hint?"

When his gaze darkened, Presley realized she'd

asked the wrong question.

"Why do you keep pushing?" His gaze locked on hers.

Presley shrugged, trying to backtrack before this escalated any further. "I was just curious. That's all. I'm sorry I asked."

"You've never been curious before." His eyes darkened, almost as if a black cloud covered them. "As a matter of fact, it almost sounds like you're questioning me."

"Alex . . . I didn't mean anything by it." She prayed he believed her, that this conversation didn't turn toxic.

She shouldn't have ever asked questions. But she'd known that.

She'd known what the outcome would be.

Yet something bigger than herself had nudged her to do so.

Presley wished she could say she'd gone numb to the pain . . . but she didn't think that would ever be a true possibility.

Because, even if she tried, Alex would just keep pushing until he got the response from her that he wanted—fear.

In fact, most of the time, fear felt like her closest companion.

Was it too late to change that?

CHAPTER
FIVE

ALEX STARED at her another moment, the muscle in his jaw twitching.

He was trying to figure out her motives, wasn't he?

Presley kept making the meat sauce, hoping he wouldn't notice her jumpiness.

But her nerves got the best of her. As she sliced a pepper, the knife slid, the blade nicking the end of her finger.

When she saw the blood, she gasped and rushed toward the sink to rinse her cut.

Alex appeared at her side. "Let me help."

"You don't have to—"

"Someone has to look out for you," he muttered. "But this is what you get."

She tensed at his reprimanding tone. "What do you mean?"

"You shouldn't have been asking questions." His tone turned terse. "And now you're facing the consequences."

"I was just asking about your life. How is that so wrong?" Why was Presley being mouthy? Usually, when Alex was in this mindset, she remained compliant. But, today, she wasn't in the mood. A rush of bravery had come from somewhere.

Or maybe it had been building up for months now. Maybe seeing Titus had brought something out in her.

She wasn't sure.

But outbursts like these always had penalties.

"If there's something you need to know about my life, I'll tell you." Alex turned the water off and pressed a paper towel over her wound. "Hold this in place."

Presley did as he said.

As her gaze sputtered to meet his, another touch of defiance flittered through her. "If you're uncomfortable with my questions, you don't have to answer. You don't have to get angry about something so trivial."

Regret . . . you're going to regret that.

Yet she couldn't seem to stop herself from retorting.

What was wrong with her?

"Oh, Presley." He reached around her waist, almost as if being sweet. But instead of stroking her hair, his fingers yanked on her locks until her head tilted back.

Her chin rose, exposing her neck.

All she could think about was the knife on the counter.

What if Alex used it?

He tugged harder, and pain stung her scalp.

Presley held her breath.

How far would Alex take this? He was generally careful, leaving any wounds hidden. He'd never broken any of her bones before—but he'd been escalating lately, and it was just a matter of time . . .

"I don't know where this sass is coming from," he muttered, examining Presley as if she were his property.

More pain stung her scalp, and her exposed neck made her limbs tremble. She wanted to reach up. Cover it. Protect herself.

But she couldn't.

"Alex . . . you're hurting me." Her voice cracked.

She could cry out for help. She had no doubt Titus

would come, but then things would get uglier than they already were.

"Now, now . . . my fingers just got tangled—maybe you need to have your hair trimmed before it gets totally unmanageable. I didn't mean any harm." He leaned closer, his lips close to her neck but never touching it. "You sound stressed, my love. You don't need to worry about anything."

She held her breath again, waiting for whatever he might do next.

Finally, he released his grip and stepped back.

She reeled as she tried to right herself.

"Hold that paper towel on your finger until it stops bleeding," he instructed as if nothing had happened.

But Presley couldn't help but wonder what he might do next—how he might decide to punish her again later.

The walls of the apartment were surprisingly thin.

Titus remained in the closet, but he could hear nearly every word coming from the kitchen.

Presley had asked Alex about The Great Awakening.

He didn't know whether to applaud her or to jump out and save her.

Especially when he heard his brother's reprimanding tone.

Titus' heart sagged when he realized that Alex wasn't going to share any information.

Then he'd heard a gasp.

He bristled. What was going on?

You shouldn't have been asking questions. And now you're facing the consequences.

Anger burned through Titus.

What kind of game was his brother playing?

Titus drew in a deep breath and then released it as he tried to get his emotions under control. His counselor had taught him what to do when his PTSD began to kick in—which it did right now.

He wanted nothing more than to jump from the space and intercede, to give his brother a piece of his mind.

But he'd promised to be quiet.

If he wanted Presley to trust him, then he needed to stay true to his word.

However, his hands fisted at his side when he heard how Alex spoke to her.

His brother had always been an arrogant jerk. But it seemed as if those qualities had only increased through the years he and Titus had been apart.

As his phone buzzed, Titus carefully pulled it from his pocket. His team leader, Brandon, was checking in to see what was happening. He'd respond later.

The glow of the screen filled the closet, its illumination catching on something shiny in the corner, stuffed into a box of sweaters.

Titus leaned down for a better look.

Was that . . . ?

Carefully, he lifted the object from its hiding space.

A gun.

Presley had a gun?

Back when they'd dated, she'd been opposed to weapons of any kind.

What had changed?

As he leaned against the wall, a crash sounded on the other side of the wall.

Titus froze.

What had just happened?

He pressed his eyes closed, praying this operation wasn't blown before it ever really started—and praying Presley wouldn't end up as collateral damage.

CHAPTER
SIX

AS A CRASH ECHOED in her apartment, Presley froze.

Her heart hammered in her ears as the seconds slowly ticked by.

Her insides quivered. Her lungs tightened.

Finally, her gaze flickered to Alex.

"What was that?" Alex narrowed his eyes as he studied her.

Presley shrugged, hoping her expression didn't show any telltale signs of Titus' presence. "I don't know. It could have been one of my neighbors."

He stepped toward the living room, his gaze dark and his shoulders tense. "That sounded like it came from inside your place."

Her throat constricted. "I don't know what it could have been."

She stepped back to the stove and gave the meat sauce a stir before it burned. Unplanned moments like that were definitely one of Alex's triggers.

What would he do next?

A small patch of sweat trickled down her back.

As he stepped toward the hallway leading to her bedrooms, her quivering nerves turned into near panic.

What if he discovered Titus?

Titus could handle himself. But when all was said and done, things would be ugly for Presley.

Really ugly.

She pressed her eyelids together. She should never have let Titus stay in her apartment.

But she had.

Then it was too late. Stuffing him in the closet had been the only solution she'd come up with.

But what if it had been a mistake?

She grabbed the butcher knife from the kitchen island and gripped it. She didn't even know why.

Was she willing to use it on Alex if it came down to it?

Presley couldn't say for sure. She only knew she felt safer with it in her hands.

If Alex asked, she could say she was chopping more onions and hadn't meant to bring it with her.

Or she could tell him she brought the knife to defend herself in case there was an intruder.

She'd decide which excuse worked best in the moment.

Alex paused in the hallway, looking back and forth between her room and the guest bedroom.

The guest bedroom, Presley silently prayed.

But almost as if he sensed the truth, Alex turned toward the primary bedroom instead.

He pushed the door open and stepped inside.

As he did, Presley held her breath, uncertain how things were about to play out.

Titus heard the floor creak.

Alex was in the bedroom, wasn't he?

Titus had a gun holstered at his waist. He would use it if necessary.

Or he could try to play this off.

But there was no way he'd be able to explain why he was hiding in Presley's closet.

Titus only prayed this didn't turn violent . . . not just for his sake. Mostly, for Presley's sake.

Even though Presley had broken his heart, Titus didn't have any ill will toward her. In fact, the thought of anything happening to her made his muscles snap tighter than a mousetrap ready to spring.

His heart continued to pound in his chest as he waited.

Footsteps strode closer.

Alex was searching the space, wasn't he? Maybe even looking under the bed.

Titus had tucked himself in the corner of the closet and dresses hung in front of him.

At first glance, someone might not see him if they opened the door.

But if Alex looked more closely . . .

"Look . . ." Presley said. "It was a picture. The frame must have fallen off the wall. I hung this one myself—not very well, obviously."

"You should have let me do it."

"I know . . . but you've been so busy."

A picture had fallen. Titus wasn't sure if he'd caused it by leaning against the wall. Had this truly been a coincidence?

If so . . . talk about poor timing.

"Why are you holding a knife?" his brother asked.

"Oh, this?" Presley let out a little laugh. "I got nervous, I guess."

There was a pause. Then, "Maybe I should check out the closet, just to be certain."

"I'm sure it was my fault—I shouldn't have used that Command Strip—"

Titus heard the handle turn.

Saw a sliver of light as the door cracked open.

This was it.

The moment everything went down.

Alex finding Titus here could ruin their mission.

Ruin their opportunity to find answers.

Ensure the fact that hundreds—or thousands—of innocent people could die.

Everything had come down to this moment.

Titus waited, his hand on his gun . . . just in case.

CHAPTER
SEVEN

She held her breath as Alex opened the closet.

At any second, he would discover Titus.

Then chaos would ensue.

Her hand went to her throat as anxiety tried to claim her.

Alex scanned the closet, not moving any clothes.

Not yet.

He only stared.

Just as he started to deepen his search, his phone rang.

She released the breath she held. But relaxing would be premature.

Alex stepped away from the closet and shoved his phone to his ear, muttering a few things into it before turning back to Presley. "I know you're making dinner, but I need to run."

"Right now? So suddenly?" Presley tried to sound disappointed, even though she was anything but.

"I'm sorry, but something came up that can't wait." He slid his phone back into his pocket and stepped toward the door. "But save the spaghetti, and maybe we can have it another time."

Presley wanted to ask him where he was going or what had come up.

But she couldn't.

Not after so many close calls already.

Instead, she trailed behind him as he walked to the door. He paused there and kissed her cheek again, the repulsing scent of his expensive, spicy cologne filling her nostrils.

"You look pretty today." He glanced her up and down as he stood in the doorway. "I like it when you wear your hair like that."

"Thank you." But she knew what he was really getting at.

Alex was really telling Presley that he wanted her to fix her hair like this more often.

Telling her how to dress and style her hair was only part of his controlling nature.

A moment later, Alex slipped out the door.

Presley locked it behind him, then waited as she

heard his footsteps fading down the hallway. She paced to the window and shoved the curtain aside—only by an inch, just in case Alex was watching—and she peered outside.

A moment later, she spotted Alex climbing into the black Lexus he'd parked at the curb, one with a license plate reading SHARK.

She waited until the headlights came on and the vehicle eased away from the curb and down the street.

Then the air whooshed from her lungs.

She glanced at her hand and noticed she was still holding the knife. It trembled in her grasp.

She practically flung it onto the end table, wanting nothing more than to collapse into the chair beside her as she recovered from what had just happened.

But she couldn't.

She needed to get Titus out of here and make sure he stayed far away—from this apartment and from her.

Titus willed himself to remain still. As soon as he heard the door close, he'd wanted to emerge from the closet and assess the situation.

But he didn't.

Instead, he waited until Presley opened the door a few moments later.

She motioned for him to come out, her actions almost frantic.

"Presley, I'm sorry," Titus started. "I didn't mean to—"

She put her hand on his arm and led him into the hallway. "You need to leave."

Titus stopped in the living room and planted his feet. "Alex is gone."

"But for how long? He could come back at any time. You can't stay."

"Presley . . . I have my guys watching the place. At the first sign that he's coming back, they'll tell me. If he does, this time I'll get out of your apartment instead of hiding."

Her shoulders seemed to slump, and her hand went to the skin between her eyes. She rubbed the spot as if fighting a headache.

When she looked back up, her tumultuous gaze wavered as it met his. "You can't be here."

"If you want me to leave, I will. But we still need to talk. I think you understand how urgent this is." There was so much Titus wanted to say. He wanted to ask what had happened while he was in the closet. If Alex had hurt her.

But first he had to convince Presley to let him stay.

She glanced up at him again, questions in her gaze. "You're sure your guys will see him if he comes back?"

"I promise."

Finally, she nodded—almost with resignation. "Fine. While you're here, you might as well have some spaghetti."

Titus had noticed the scent of garlic and onions floating through the air. He wasn't particularly hungry, but they needed to talk.

He followed her into the kitchen, hoping he might be able to gain some answers and prevent a needless tragedy.

CHAPTER
EIGHT

THIS WAS A BAD IDEA. Presley should have told Titus to leave.

But now she was curious.

And worried.

Maybe she'd been in denial for too long. If Alex and his friends really were planning some type of terrorist attack, she couldn't just sit back and do nothing.

Even if that meant sacrificing her own safety.

She tried to swallow the lump in her throat but ended up coughing instead.

She wanted to believe she was strong and courageous. But she hadn't even managed to end her relationship with Alex for fear of his wrath.

No, brave was the last way Presley would

describe herself. She'd been tested and saw the truth about herself.

But maybe it wasn't too late to change that.

After putting a Band-Aid over the cut on her finger, she set a plate of spaghetti in front of Titus. Then she picked up her own food and sat across from him at the table. He'd already grabbed some water for them as well as silverware.

As she glanced at the otherwise barren table, panic raced through her. "I'm sorry. I should have made a salad or some bread—"

Titus raised his hand. "You don't have to apologize to me, Presley."

Her glazed eyes fluttered to meet his.

That's right . . . Titus wasn't Alex.

Titus wasn't prone to fits. Or to using his fists when things didn't go his way.

As she composed herself, Presley stared at the food in front of her. Even though she'd given herself a hearty portion, she knew she wouldn't be eating much. She didn't have an appetite. Too many things were on her mind.

As soon as they finished their meal, she'd need to wash the plates and put them away, just so she didn't forget later. She had to cover her tracks.

She glanced at Titus again as memories of their first date flooded back to her mind.

Memories of the Italian restaurant he'd taken her to. How they'd started talking about places they wanted to travel and ways they'd flubbed up while trying to get their first jobs.

They'd ended up laughing like two teenagers.

When Titus had kissed her that night, Presley had known she was under his spell.

Until everything had changed.

She frowned at the memories. Guilt pummeled her—guilt and regret.

But this wasn't the time to think about that.

Their past relationship wasn't why Titus had come.

Her gaze met his as she tried to focus her thoughts. "Tell me what your proposal is. I want to hear it."

Titus lowered his fork onto the table in order to give this conversation his full attention.

He'd come here with a plan, but now he realized that it wouldn't work. He needed to recalculate, and he hoped his teammates would understand when he explained things later.

"As I said before, I need someone on the inside," Titus said. "At first, I wanted that person to be you."

"I figured that but . . ." She shook her head. "I told you, I don't know much."

"I was going to try to convince you to learn more."

Her eyes widened as if the thought terrified her.

"But I changed my mind. *I* want to be that inside person now."

"You? How exactly do you plan on doing that?" Presley stared at him as though he'd lost his mind.

"I'm going to talk to Alex."

Her eyes widened even more. "You think your brother is just going to let you into the group with open arms after the two of you haven't spoken in two years?"

"Probably not. Not easily. But I'll think of a way to get in." Titus' jaw hardened as he thought through the possibilities. There had to be some way to both get answers and keep Presley safe.

"I think you're underestimating how difficult that would be." She wiped her mouth with her napkin, even though she'd barely touched her food. "I don't think you understand who these people are, Titus. Powerful people are involved with this. People with far more influence than the average person. They're the ones calling the shots. Everyone else is just a minion."

"That's why it's a better idea if I go in. I don't

want you to be our mole. I can see now that was a bad idea."

She stared at him another moment as if still processing their conversation. "So, you don't need my help then?"

"Actually, I still do. I could use someone to watch my back, to let me know if things go south so I can have a decent chance of survival. Maybe you could even warm Alex up to the idea of me getting involved."

"He doesn't listen to me." She pressed her lips together as if the admission pained her.

Titus wondered what she meant by that. Then again, he could totally see his brother dismissing her. The man was arrogant, to say the least. He wasn't the type to value Presley for her smarts or skills—only her looks and idol-like worship of him.

Alex had always dated women who didn't ask many questions, who didn't undermine his decisions. He'd called it a matter of respect on their part.

Titus used to get so angry with his brother about the way he treated women as second-class citizens. But Titus couldn't change Alex's mind. In fact, their father had been the same way. Thankfully, his mom had shielded Titus from the man as much as possible.

Presley remained silent a moment before finally nodding. "Okay. I'll do it."

"Just like that?" Titus didn't want to sound surprised, nor did he want to change her mind.

But he hadn't expected Presley to jump on board like this, especially after she'd been so hesitant earlier.

"I'm sure," she told him. "If Alex is planning what you say he is, then I have to do whatever I can to help stop it."

Titus leaned closer. "You know this could be dangerous."

"I know. But I've been living in fear for too long. It's time to make a change."

Titus stared at her another moment, wondering exactly what was behind her words.

Living in fear? What had Alex done to her? Put her through?

At once, he realized what a mistake it may have been when he'd written both Presley and Alex out of his life.

Before he could ruminate on the realization, his phone buzzed.

Brandon, his team leader, had texted to ask if they could talk.

Titus dialed Brandon's number before putting the phone to his ear.

"There's a guy out here watching Presley's apartment."

Titus' back muscles stiffened. "Who is he?"

"We can't tell. We ran his plates, but it's a rental car."

"Do you think Alex sent the guy?"

"It's hard to say. But you need to be careful." Brandon's breath caught. "This guy just got out of the car. He's heading toward the apartment building."

"What?" Titus bristled as he rose to his feet.

"And he has a gun."

CHAPTER
NINE

"STAND BY," Titus said.

Presley leaned closer, hanging onto Titus' every word as she tried to interpret the one-sided conversation.

What was happening?

Trouble was near. She was certain of it.

Was Alex back?

Her entire body stiffened at the thought. If Alex came back again, certainly he'd find Titus this time.

What would Presley tell him? Her lie would be obvious.

"I'll handle this." As Titus strode toward the door, he pulled the phone from his ear, put it on speaker, and tapped something on his screen. "I installed a camera at the end of this hallway."

He'd installed a camera outside her apartment?

Presley's mind continued to race.

Just how long had he been watching her?

What other extremes had he gone to?

She shifted uncomfortably.

"This guy is coming our way," Titus continued. "Are you getting the feed?"

"I am," a deep voice said through the phone speaker. "I'll keep an eye on it."

"I don't like the looks of this guy." Titus frowned as he looked at the screen. "But at least his gun is still holstered."

Gun? Had he said gun?

Presley paced closer, anxious to know more details. "Titus . . ."

He locked gazes with her. "I'm going to need you to answer the door."

A shiver raced up her spine as she wondered who would be on the other side. "But . . ."

"I'll be right here, hiding behind the door, and out of sight. I know you don't want anyone to see you with me right now. Until we know who this guy is . . ."

"But the gun . . ."

"I'm keeping my eye on him. At the first sign he's reaching for it, I'll protect you. I promise."

Presley's thoughts started to spiral toward fear, but she forced herself to stop them. Instead, she nodded, using every ounce of her strength to remain calm. "Okay then."

As the words left her lips, a knock sounded at the door.

She glanced at Titus again, and he nodded.

Then he pointed to the area behind the door, indicating he'd be waiting there.

His presence made her feel a little better. But still . . .

As she paced toward the door, Titus got into position and withdrew his gun.

His gun?

Presley's throat tightened until she could hardly breathe.

She didn't like guns . . . but she'd bought one for herself a month ago.

Just in case.

But she prayed she'd never have to use it.

Leaving the chain lock in place, she cracked the door open.

The man on the other side stared at her.

Calculating brown eyes. Messy brown hair. Disheveled appearance.

Fear shot up her spine like lightning during a storm.

Who was this guy?

Had he been sent here to hurt her?

Titus gripped his gun, praying he didn't have to use it.

But he would if he had to.

He had no idea who the guy on the other side of the door was or where this situation was going.

"Can I help you?" Presley asked.

"Good evening." A slight Texas twang captured the man's voice, and the lazy tone made him sound friendly despite his uninvited presence. "I'm sorry to disturb you, but I'm Jesse—I don't live far from here. I just got home and noticed someone parked on the street had left their car lights on."

Titus didn't remember seeing that when he'd glanced out the window.

"I appreciate your vigilance, but my car isn't parked on the street," Presley muttered.

"It's probably smarter that it's not." He shrugged. "I just thought I'd let you know, just in case."

"I appreciate that, but . . . why did you assume it was mine? Or are you hitting all the apartments in this building?"

The man chuckled. "No, yours is the only one with a light on. I figured . . . well, I figured I'd appreciate it if someone did it for me."

Presley's shoulders visibly relaxed at the explanation. "Of course. Have a good evening."

"You as well."

Presley closed the door and turned to Titus, looking more at ease now.

He almost hated to burst her bubble.

"I don't know who that guy is, but he's more than a concerned neighbor."

A knot formed on her brow. "Why do you say that?"

"Because he's been watching your apartment for the past thirty minutes."

CHAPTER
TEN

PRESLEY LOWERED herself into the chair at the dining room table, feeling as if her legs might not hold her up.

She stared at the spaghetti in front of her. The dish was cold and basically untouched. She had no desire to eat.

Titus seemed to sense she needed space. He collected their plates, disposing of the leftovers. Then he washed the dishes, dried them, and put them away.

When he was done, he sat beside her. Resting his elbows against his legs, he leaned forward, still waiting patiently.

How could two brothers be so different?

And how could she have been so wrong?

Sometimes Presley liked to think about how

things might have turned out differently if Alex hadn't convinced her to leave Titus. Would she be happy now? Maybe even thriving?

She glanced up at Titus.

They were wasting time, and his presence here was risky. Even though Titus said his friends were outside keeping an eye on things, Alex was sly. She wouldn't put it past him to slip by and make it up to her apartment without anyone noticing.

But if what Titus had told her was true . . .

She released a long breath. "If you want to infiltrate The System, I know I can't stop you," she finally said. "But you're putting yourself in a very dangerous position. You have no idea who you're dealing with. These people look innocent and kind on the outside. But once you get past those façades, you're staring at soulless people lacking even an ounce of compassion."

"You shouldn't be around people like that either." Titus stared into her eyes as if he could see through them into her soul.

The look caused a lump to form in her throat. She quickly swallowed, trying not to choke on her emotions. "It's too late for me."

"Is it? Maybe I could—"

She stood and started to walk away. She couldn't stand the hope in his voice.

As she did, Titus stood and grabbed her arm.

Instinct kicked in, and she recoiled.

Worst-case scenarios flashed through her mind as memories pummeled her.

And she braced herself for the repercussions of walking away from the conversation without being dismissed.

As Titus saw Presley cowering, he froze.

Quickly, he released her arm. He hadn't meant to cause that kind of reaction.

Then realization hit him.

She'd recoiled in fear. Like a dog who'd been beaten.

Anger turned his blood into lava.

He fisted his hands at his side before releasing them, not wanting to scare Presley any more than she already was.

"My brother's been hitting you, hasn't he?" Titus stared into her eyes, unable to look away as anger burned through his veins. He needed to see the truth. He needed to know if his suspicions were correct.

Presley straightened, but her gaze looked fragile. Even though she held herself steady, something broken still remained about her. "Hitting is a strong word—"

"Don't downplay whatever it is he's done to you. Don't try to cover for him. If my brother is—"

"It doesn't matter." Emotion flared in her gaze. "It is what it is."

Titus stepped closer, knowing he couldn't drop this yet. "It *does* matter. If Alex is hurting you, then you need to get away."

She raised her chin, even as moisture glimmered in her gaze "I've already tried. Twice. Both times he stopped me."

His chest squeezed until he felt like his heart might be crushed.

He tried to imagine everything Presley had been through, but the thoughts made him sick to his stomach.

How could Titus have let this happen? He should have never put distance between them.

All he'd ever wanted to do was to protect her.

When the two of them had first met, Presley had been handing out sunscreen samples on the beach in the resort area of Virginia Beach. It seemed as if being beautiful and engaging was a prerequisite for the job.

Titus had just gotten in from surfing, and he was drying off when he noticed the commotion several feet away.

A man was getting aggressive with Presley. Had tried to touch her when his touch hadn't been welcome.

Titus had intervened and quickly put the man in his place. But Presley was shaken from the encounter. Titus had pulled her aside to make sure she was okay.

After talking for a few minutes, he'd taken her to get a smoothie in hopes of calming her down.

They were inseparable afterward.

Until Alex.

Titus frowned and reminded himself that it was too late to go back now.

But he could stop Alex from hurting her again in the future.

"I know what you're thinking." Presley shook her head vehemently as her gaze locked with his. "Don't get involved, Titus."

Titus' shoulders stiffened. "I can't stand by and let Alex do this to you."

She kept shaking her head. "I appreciate the fact you want to help, but I'm in too deep. Now, I'm not only in too deep with Alex, but I'm in too deep with The System."

"Then you're already on the inside?" Titus held his breath as he waited for her answer.

"Not really. I'm just a foot soldier. But they won't let me walk away. They don't let *anyone* walk away."

More anger surged through Titus.

There had to be something he could do.

But every possibility would ruin this operation.

From the intel they'd gathered, hundreds of thousands of lives were on the line.

Could Titus really ignore those people and choose instead to save the only woman he'd ever loved?

The answer should be easy, but it wasn't. It was anything but.

Presley stared at him, anxiety in her gaze as she waited for his reply.

CHAPTER
ELEVEN

PRESLEY COULDN'T WAIT for Titus any longer. "Before I get cold feet, we need to talk about this plan you mentioned."

She'd never intended on letting him know how vulnerable she was. Or how weak. But something about seeing his concern had caused the reaction. Plus, she was already on edge.

Titus stared at her another moment as if assessing her mental state before finally nodding. "Okay. I know we don't have a lot of time to go through things. But I need to know everything you can tell me about The System. I already checked your apartment for bugs. You're clear."

"You thought my apartment was bugged?"

He shrugged. "It was a possibility."

She shoved her nerves aside at the thought and

pushed a hair behind her ear before nodding toward the table beside them. "Okay. Let's talk."

As they sat beside each other, the air seemed to crackle with tension between them.

Presley cleared her throat. She'd come this far. She'd taken the first step.

But this was the hard part. "What exactly do you need to know?"

Titus hesitated only a moment before saying, "The System's schedule. Where they meet. When. Who they are. Anything you can tell me will help."

She pushed away another flash of fear. Even talking to Titus . . . it was reason enough for The System to make her suffer a steep penalty.

And by steep penalty, Presley knew they would make her pay—with her reputation, her money, her relationships. Wherever they could hit her the hardest.

Titus had said someone who'd been willing to talk had died of a supposed heart attack. She knew that wasn't the case. He'd been killed.

What about that man outside? Why had he come up here? Was he still watching her place?

Was he watching *her*?

There were so many unknowns and uncertainties.

Presley drew in a deep breath as she pulled her thoughts together.

"Alex got involved with this group about two years ago, right about the time we—" Presley couldn't finish the sentence.

She almost said, *right about the time we broke up.* But this didn't seem like the occasion to broach that subject.

Titus' gaze darkened. "Go on."

"Alex went to some type of retreat with a few of his law school buddies. Apparently, while he was there, someone told him about this new organization that was forming. A week or two later, he went to another meeting. When he came back that time, he was totally enthusiastic about what this group stood for and what they were trying to do. I don't remember ever seeing him so excited. Alex said he finally found something that he could believe in."

Titus tilted his head, his expression still stony. "Did Alex say what exactly he was so excited about believing in?"

That conversation flashed back into Presley's mind. Alex had gone on and on about The System for hours—while not ever really sharing anything specific. Her eyes had been glazing over, but she'd tried not to show it.

"He said these people had ideas—*brilliant* ideas. He said this country has been due for a change for a long time, and members of this group were the kind who had the smarts, money, and power to make it happen."

Titus narrowed his gaze as he listened. "Did he name names?"

"No, not that I remember. But, over the course of the next several months, I got to know some of the second-tier people involved. Most of them are pretty similar to Alex. They're professional. They excel in their careers. They're smart. They're not people who would raise any eyebrows."

"Did you meet any of the core leaders?"

"If I did, I wasn't aware of it. But there are five or so in the core group . These people never show their faces. I found a paper once that addressed each of them by a nickname—Member X, for example. Meeting in person is probably too risky." She shrugged. "I've never been told who they are, but I assume that Alex knows. He seems to have worked his way up the ranks pretty quickly."

"When you say that, it makes me think that, at some point, you realized these guys were up to no good. When did you put that together?"

Presley drew in a deep breath before exhaling. Memories pummeled her thoughts. Memories of her twinges of suspicion. Memories of whispered conversations. Of feeling a new excitement in the air. Of suspecting there were secrets she wasn't privy to.

"About eight months ago, at one of their meetings, I noticed they were stockpiling some strange supplies," she said. "About that time Alex started to get jumpy. He was still excited about the idea of this organization, but he also seemed agitated and preoccupied. I caught him online one time researching water reservoirs."

Titus' eyes widened with interest. "Water reservoirs? Did you ask him about it?"

"I did." She rubbed her arm as she remembered that conversation. "It didn't go well."

Titus glanced at her, seeming to put together what had happened after her question—how Presley had been punished.

His gaze darkened even more.

"I've heard there are about four thousand members of The System," he muttered. "Does that sound right to you?"

"I've heard that number thrown out also. On top of the core group, there are probably twenty leaders who really act more as advisers. The rest of the members . . . they're more like a militia waiting for orders."

Lines of worry crinkled the skin around his eyes. "Militia? Tell me more."

She sighed before saying, "There are other people involved who never come to meetings. They connect with each other online instead. The System is always trying to network and expand their membership. The leaders are salesmen. They know how to pitch their beliefs to make it sound like they're doing something noble and good."

"But you knew they were up to no good?"

"I've had a bad feeling about them. But not to the extent you mentioned. If what you're saying is true . . . I don't think violence is the way to make changes. There are better ways."

Titus leaned closer. "Do you know when they're meeting again?"

"As a matter of fact, I do. In two days—on Saturday morning."

Titus didn't want to leave Presley.

Especially when he thought about what his brother had done to her.

But, right now, his hands were tied. Alex could return at any moment. The longer Titus stayed, the more Presley would be at risk. He couldn't do that to her.

He rose from his seat and glanced around the kitchen one more time to confirm there was no evidence he'd been here.

Presley stood also and paused in front of him, looking just as beautiful as ever.

She was so gorgeous.

Titus had felt like the luckiest man in the world to have her on his arm.

He'd fallen fast and hard.

In fact, he'd never gotten over her. He hadn't connected with anyone at the same level—and he didn't think he ever would.

"What are you going to do now?"

Presley's soft voice pulled him from his thoughts. "I'm going to figure out a way to get into my brother's good graces and become a part of The System."

She lowered her gaze as if she didn't like that idea. "Do you really think your brother is going to forgive you that easily?"

"Forgive *me*? *I'm* the one angry with *him*. *He's* the one who stole *my* girlfriend while I was deployed." He tried to hide the bitter edge to his voice, but it didn't work.

Presley opened her mouth as if to speak before closing it again. She nodded instead. "That's all I can tell you right now. But if I think of anything else—"

"Can you memorize my number? The line is untraceable. It will just look like I'm some type of robo caller if the number pops up in your call list."

"I can remember it."

Titus rattled off the digits. "If you need me for anything, call me. On second thought, memorize my address as well." He told her the information.

"Got it. Do you need my number?"

A grin tried to tug at his lips, but this situation didn't warrant any smiles. "I already have it."

Her eyes widened before she quickly lowered her lids. "I should have known."

Titus lingered another minute, wanting to say more but knowing there was nothing else to say. With a nod to Presley, he strode to the door.

"I'll see you later, Presley."

"Good night, Titus."

Something about the way she said his name made his heart give an involuntary pitter-patter.

He glanced at his phone—and checked the camera in her hallway—to make sure that no one was around. Then he slipped out and closed the door behind him. Once he heard the lock click in place, he started down the hallway.

When he reached the first floor, he slipped out a back exit. He walked toward the sidewalk out front and paused in the shadows.

The late spring weather felt oppressive—humid and heavy, even though the temperature was only in the low eighties. Although, right now, his warmth might be because of the situation.

Titus surveyed the area and spotted Brandon in his SUV. He also saw a car with a silhouette inside.

The man who'd come to the door was still here. Still watching.

What did he say his name was? Jesse?

What did that man want?

In other circumstances, Titus might storm toward the man's car and demand some answers.

But, right now, he needed to keep a low profile.

Hopefully, his team members could figure out who Jesse was. Maybe run his image through a facial recognition system. Or trace the license plate back to the rental company to figure out who had signed for the vehicle. There was more than one way to skin a cat, as his grandfather had told him.

Titus stayed in the shadows as he walked to his car.

Tomorrow would be another hard day.

And Titus needed to get ready for it.

CHAPTER
TWELVE

THE NEXT MORNING, Presley looked up from her computer as someone knocked at her office door.

It was Jeannine Bluefield, Alex's secretary. A pensive expression stretched across the fifty-something woman's already drawn features. "Mr. Armstrong would like to see you."

Presley's spine stiffened as she sat at her desk in her small office. Why had Alex sent Jeannine to get her instead of calling her himself?

Jeannine seemed to read her thoughts. "I just finished a meeting with him, and he asked if I could come get you."

Based on the tightness to her words, the meeting had been tense.

Alex was always polite at work. But when things became busy, he could get intense. If anyone else here could sense that rigid control in Alex, it was Jeannine.

Presley wondered if her own expression often mirrored Jeannine's. The same trepidation about what might happen next if she displeased Alex. The subtle put-downs. The gaslighting. The stonewalling.

Presley rose and glanced at a mirror she kept beside her desk. Quickly, she touched up her lip gloss.

The fewer things she gave Alex to criticize her about, the better.

Smoothing her skirt, she ambled down the hallway toward Alex's office.

He'd gotten her this job as an administrative assistant here at his law firm. Of course, he said it wouldn't be appropriate if she worked directly for him. So, instead, she worked for one of his colleagues.

But that didn't stop him from asking her to do things for him.

Presley knew why Alex had brought her into the company.

He wanted to keep an eye on her. That was the only reason he wanted her to work here.

After all, before this, her summertime job had been acting as a spokesperson for a sunscreen company. In the winter, she'd been a tour guide for a resort.

Presley stepped into his expansive office and offered a smile. "What's going on?"

"You look nice." Alex looked her up and down with approval. "Come in and shut the door."

A shiver ran through her. But Presley did as he said.

"Have a seat." He nodded toward the chair across from him.

Again, Presley did as he said and then waited for him to continue.

"I have something I need to have picked up today."

"Okay . . ." She wondered why he was telling her this. "Would you like for me to arrange an office courier to pick it up for you?"

His cheek flickered. "Actually, I'd like for you to pick the package up. I need someone I trust to oversee it."

A rumble of nerves raced through her. "It sounds . . . important."

He shrugged as if it weren't a big deal. "Just sentimental stuff—some old uniforms belonging to my grandfather. I had them cleaned and pressed to preserve them. I've already paid, so you'd just need to pick them up. Ask for Kenneth."

His grandfather's old uniforms? Alex *did* seem fond of his grandfather, but this whole explanation didn't ring true to her.

Regardless, Presley knew she didn't really have a choice. "Of course. I'd be more than happy to."

"That's my girl." He pushed a piece of paper across the desk. "Here's the address. It's close enough you can walk—and it's a beautiful day outside."

"Walking sounds nice. I can leave now if you'd like."

"That would be perfect. Thank you."

Alex's phone buzzed. As he clicked on it, Jeannine's voice filled the room. "Mr. Armstrong . . . there's someone here to see you."

His gaze darkened. "I don't have any meetings scheduled."

"I know, sir. But he says . . . he's your brother."

As Titus stood in the lobby of Armstrong and Associates, he mentally rehearsed his cover story. His teammates had come to his apartment last night, and they'd gone over his spiel several times until the story felt natural.

Right now, Titus wore a black T-shirt with his

favorite jeans. Dressing up too much might seem suspicious. It didn't fit his normal MO.

As he waited, he glanced around the office.

With its polished marble floor and walls, no expense had been spared. Everything looked pristine and clean. The air even smelled purified.

It fit his brother. He'd always liked trophies. In high school and college, the trophies had been literal awards for his achievements in academics and sports. But as he'd gotten older, those things had turned into expensive cars, stately houses, prestigious titles.

Beautiful girlfriends.

Titus frowned.

He imagined Presley working here—Presley, a girl who'd loved nothing more than living in a swimsuit and flipflops. Who'd loved wearing her hair long and flowing down her back. Who'd ordered the cheapest thing on the menu because money was tight and who'd preferred homestyle diners to elegant restaurants.

The two of them had bonded over bodysurfing in the ocean. They had taken it upon themselves to try every flavor of ice cream they could find and had listened to free concerts on the beach whenever possible.

He frowned at the memories. Not because they

weren't good ones. But because he'd wanted more of them.

Titus sighed as he tried to gather his thoughts.

He found comfort in knowing that one of his teammates had remained outside Presley's last night to keep an eye on things. Alex hadn't returned.

But Jesse—or whatever that man's real name was —had also remained in front of Presley's apartment. Blackout had been unable to find out the man's identity through their normal means. But they were still working on it.

A terse-looking woman with a tight bun paused outside the door. "Mr. Armstrong will see you now."

Titus sucked in a deep breath, praying he'd be able to pull this off.

Then he followed her down the hallway toward Alex's office, ready to put on the show of his life.

CHAPTER
THIRTEEN

TITUS WATCHED as Alex rose from his seat. Just as when they'd been kids, something about his brother made him seem like a giant. He was only two inches taller than Titus' six-foot frame, and he wasn't as broad.

Yet Alex was larger than life, full of himself, and he knew his presence could fill a room.

"You're the last person I expected to see." His brother fiddled with a button on his jacket before sitting down. "Have a seat."

Titus glanced at Presley and gave her a nod, trying to act as if they hadn't seen each other in years—since she broke his heart. "Presley."

She nodded back. "Titus."

A certain coolness drifted between them.

Was it an act? Or was the feeling real?

He wasn't sure.

"What brings you by?" Alex asked.

Titus cleared his throat and turned back to his brother. "I'm back in town so I thought I should look you up."

"It's been a long time." Alex studied him with open curiosity, clearly not anxious to make the first move.

"It has." Titus swallowed hard. "I thought it was time to make things right."

"What happened to cause this change of heart? Perhaps, something life-altering?"

"You could say that. I was on a mission when an IED exploded only fifteen feet away. One of our guys didn't make it. I was one of the lucky ones, but the blast blew my knee out. The injury killed my career as a SEAL. Anyway, when that happened, it made me realize how important family is." The words tasted bitter as they came from Titus' mouth.

He really had lost someone on the SEAL team due to an IED explosion. And that fact really had given him a greater appreciation for the people in his life.

But Alex hadn't made that list.

At this moment, Titus needed to act as if he had.

"I'm sorry to hear about your friend, but I'm glad you came by. I regret the way that things ended between us." Alex glanced at Presley. "Both of us do. Right, my love?"

The way his brother said the endearment sounded more obsessive than sweet.

Presley shifted, crossing and uncrossing her legs as if nervous. "Of course . . . we never intended for this to happen."

Maybe *Presley* hadn't intended for it to happen, but Alex had. He'd had his sights on Presley from the day they'd first met—while Titus was dating her.

Alex had come into town for business and asked Titus to have dinner with him. Titus had brought Presley. From the moment his brother had seen her, he'd been on his best behavior, transforming from persnickety and critical to charming and engaging.

"What are you doing now?" Alex leaned back in his chair, looking entirely too casual. "Are you in the military in a non-SEAL capacity?"

"No, I left the service six months ago." Titus shrugged. "The whole experience wasn't what I thought it would be. I guess I was becoming disillusioned, and I figured it was better to get out than to let anger build inside me over the direction I saw things going."

Titus saw the flicker of interest in Alex's eyes.

If Titus played his cards right, he may just hook this assignment after all.

Alex glanced at Presley, ownership in his gaze. "Why don't you go do that errand I asked you to do for me? We'll meet up later."

Presley stole one more glance at Titus before nodding and rising. "Of course. You two enjoy catching up."

Then she was gone.

When she left, she took every ounce of goodness and hope with her from the room.

Presley felt another surge of anxiety.

Why did she always feel so anxious? So jumpy? Like she was always on edge?

It was no way to live. Yet, she felt helpless to change it.

If there was one thing she hated, it was feeling helpless. She'd had a lifetime of that growing up with her mother pushing her into the pageant world—not for Presley's sake, but for her mom's.

The connections her mom had made on the pageant circuit had garnered her mother three different husbands—all of whom had left before being married a year. Maybe that was why her mother had somehow found her own self-worth in Presley's accomplishments.

Resisting her mom only got her into trouble, and Presley had learned to stay quiet and compliant. She'd carried those lessons on with her into adulthood.

Maybe that's why Alex had pursued her. Compliance was what he demanded. He was a predator who could sniff out weakness a mile away.

Snapping back to the present, she grabbed her purse from her office before starting outside on this errand Alex had insisted only she could do.

She didn't like the sound of that.

But Alex thought he could control Presley so much that she'd do whatever he asked without batting an eyelash.

That's what she wanted him to believe. Because if Alex believed anything else, then pain would follow.

So, Presley had learned the skill of pretending to be fine as a coping mechanism.

She sighed and checked the address Alex had given her again. She took the elevator down and then stepped onto the sidewalk.

As soon as she was outside, her spine stiffened.

Presley glanced around.

That man who'd come to her apartment last night . . . was he nearby right now? Was he blending in with the crowds as he watched her?

Her gut told her yes.

She glanced at the people on the sidewalk, at the cars parked along the side of the street, but she didn't see him. It had been so dark outside last night . . . there were no guarantees she'd even recognize his vehicle if she saw it.

Her steps quickened as a new sense of urgency filled the air.

What if Alex suspected she'd been talking to Titus? What if he sent her on this errand just so he could stage some type of accident?

Terror shimmied through her.

She continued walking three blocks until she reached Winston's Dry Cleaning.

As she stepped inside the dirty establishment, she paused. This didn't seem like the type of place Alex would normally use. He was too immaculate for a place with a grimy floor and a peeling laminate countertop. The strong chemical scent of solvent filled the air, mixed with the aroma of fried foods.

But it wasn't her job to ask questions.

Instead, Presley strode toward the counter. An Asian woman glanced at her from over the rim of her glasses, waiting for Presley to initiate the conversation.

"I need to talk to Kenneth," Presley started.

"Who are you?" The woman's words sounded brisk, almost impatient.

"Presley. He should be expecting me."

The clerk pushed her glasses up higher on her nose and observed Presley another minute. Presley apparently passed her test because the woman ambled through a door at the back of the storefront.

A moment later, a short, balding man with light brown skin introduced himself as Kenneth. Without saying anything else, he handed her a box the size of a carry-on suitcase. The sides were made of a slick, plastic-like cardboard and packing tape sealed the folds.

As soon as it was in Presley's hands, he turned and disappeared into the back again, almost as if the exchange had never happened.

Another rush of nerves shot up Presley's spine.

What had she just picked up?

Even more than that, what had she just implicated herself in?

Her throat tightened as she stepped outside.

If what Titus had told her was true, the contents of this box could be something that related to the domestic terrorist incident that might be taking place in four days.

What if, by delivering this box, Presley was in some way helping to pull off the act?

How could she live with herself if that was the case?

She already knew the answer to that question.

She couldn't.

She scanned the city streets and sidewalks around her, still feeling unseen eyes on her.

Right now, she needed to find a place she could be alone.

A fast-food restaurant across the street caught her eye.

Burger Feast had a storefront here, complete with a bright yellow-and-red sign and a line of people out the door.

Moving swiftly and purposefully, Presley slipped inside and walked directly to a bathroom.

Thankfully, it was a single occupancy room.

She locked the door before setting the box on the sink.

Her heart raced as she stared at it.

What was she doing here?

But she knew.

She couldn't keep being someone's puppet.

Seeing Titus had ignited something inside her—the need for change.

The need to take back control of her life. To be the person she'd started to become while dating Titus. He'd given her the courage to be herself instead of trying to be someone who simply made others happy.

She'd vanished in recent years. She'd accepted that as her fate, her punishment almost.

Not any longer.

Presley swallowed hard as she tugged at the packing tape.

It peeled off, the slick sides of the box remaining intact.

Perfect.

With trembling hands, she opened the folds.

Her heart throbbed in her ears as she waited to see what was inside.

CHAPTER
FOURTEEN

PRESLEY'S HANDS trembled as she pulled the box flaps open.

She halfway expected to find a bomb inside—even though she knew the package would be heavier if that were the case. No, whatever was inside felt soft and fairly lightweight.

Some uniforms had been folded inside the box, just as Alex said.

But why were they in a box?

At first glance, she wondered if Alex's grandfather had been a cop. Maybe Alex *had* been telling the truth.

But as she pulled a uniform from the box, she realized this style was entirely too modern to have been his grandfather's.

This looked like a current-day police uniform.

That's when it hit her.

The System needed to disguise someone as a cop.

Alarm raced through her.

The bathroom doorknob rattled then pounding sounded. "How much longer?" a deep voice demanded from the other side. "I gotta go!"

Presley dropped the uniform onto the grimy floor before quickly snatching it back up. As her blood pressure rose, her heart pounded in her ears. "One minute!"

Presley glanced through the rest of the box. There were three uniforms altogether. Each seemed to be a perfect replica of an actual police uniform, something no one would question if they saw someone wearing it in public.

Domestic terrorist attack.

She couldn't stop thinking about Titus' words. Thinking about the innocent lives that could be lost.

Presley couldn't have any part of that. She *couldn't.*

But if she delivered these uniforms to Alex, wasn't that exactly what she'd be doing?

Think quickly. What can you do?

Presley began searching through her purse.

That's when she found her answer.

A small bottle of nail polish remover.

She'd brought it with her to work today because

she'd considered doing her nails on her lunch break. One time a chip in her nail had set Alex off. She'd learned since then to take better care of her appearance. Every little detail mattered.

As she unscrewed the top to the bottle, she paused.

If she did this, there would be no going back.

She hesitated as nausea roiled in her stomach.

As Presley stared at the uniforms, the man pounded on the door again.

She flinched at the sound.

As she did, drops of remover splashed from the bottle.

Her chest tightened.

Two small dots formed on the collar of the uniform.

Presley pressed her eyes closed. She prayed she knew what she was doing, but she knew that she didn't. She had no idea what kind of consequences this would have.

"Lady! Can you hurry up?" the man on the other side of the door continued.

"I'll be out soon!" she called back.

Presley couldn't put too much of this remover in the box. If she did, Alex would smell it.

Instead, she tilted it until a few more drips hit the collars.

No self-respecting cop would wear a uniform with visible bleach stains.

Quickly, she stashed her bottle back in her purse and then closed the box. She washed her hands, trying to get rid of the scent of the nail polish remover—just in case.

Then she carefully pressed the tape back in place on the box edges.

She needed to get to the office before too much time had passed and Alex began to ask questions.

But Presley may have just written her own death certificate.

"So, you said you were becoming disillusioned with the military?" Alex leaned back in his chair, still observing Titus with interest as they talked in his office.

Titus remembered the spiel he'd put together before coming, a script he'd quickly memorized. "You could say that. Things just aren't the way they used to be. I know I'm probably too young to say that. But even I could see the shift, and I knew I had to get out before something bad happened."

Approval gleamed in Alex's eyes. "Some people

think this country is in shambles and that our government needs a major overhaul."

"I can see why they'd think that. After I got back from deployment, it was easy to see. Things had changed in that short time. I wasn't even proud to serve my country anymore." Titus' words weren't true. Serving his country had brought Titus the utmost pride and a real sense of fulfillment.

But he couldn't tell Alex that. He needed his brother to believe they could possibly hold the same viewpoints.

Alex grunted as if processing what Titus told him.

Finally, his brother nodded. "I'm really glad you came by, Titus. Have you found another job now that you've entered civilian life?"

"Not yet. But with my skills, I'm hoping something will open up—maybe something else in security. I did work briefly for another organization, but it didn't work out. All those guys . . . they were just like the ones I left behind in the military. They didn't seem to see or mind the changes like I did. I couldn't take it anymore."

Titus had to throw that tidbit in since on his last assignment, he'd worked as security for someone who'd inadvertently been connected to The System. Titus had no doubt his brother could easily find out that information if he tried.

"I might have an idea of a job for you." Alex shifted in his seat

Titus perked, careful not to seem too eager. "I didn't come here to ask you for a job."

"You didn't ask. I could use a guy like you." Alex nodded again as if his idea was settling in. "I don't want to talk about it here, though. Can you meet for dinner tonight? I need to do it earlier than usual."

"I'm intrigued. I'd be willing to hear you out."

Alex shifted forward, a new look gleaming in his gaze. "I'm really glad you came here, Titus, and that you've put the past behind you. That means the world to me. About the way things went down after Presley's mom died . . ."

Titus kept his expression even, neutral—careful not to show any of his real emotions. "I was on deployment. I know Presley was struggling, and I couldn't be there for her."

Alex shrugged. "I didn't expect to feel such a strong connection or for things to develop as they did. I suppose the heart wants what the heart wants."

"I guess so." Titus swallowed hard as he tried to calm the rage flaring to life inside him. He hated himself for pretending like this was all okay.

He hadn't known about Presley's loss until two weeks after the fact. He'd been unreachable on a classified mission.

By the time he'd gotten her message, it was too late.

Alex had taken advantage of her in her time of need.

None of it was okay.

But there was nothing Titus could do about it right now—nothing beneficial to this mission, at least.

"Give my secretary your info, and I'll have her text the place we can meet," Alex finally said, shifting again in his seat. "We can catch up more then. Would it bother you if I brought Presley with me?"

"Not at all." Titus would do his best to forgive and forget.

All that resentment . . . it could make a person do something he might regret.

And Titus already had a list of regrets a mile long.

BY THE TIME Presley got back to the office, she felt like a hot mess.

Nothing had happened on her way back to work, but she couldn't shake the feeling she was being watched, followed.

Although she still didn't know why someone would want to do that.

She hadn't done anything to raise any alarms.

But these people who were part of The System . . . they valued loyalty. They valued people who didn't ask questions or disturb the status quo—even though that's what they were doing themselves with the country's political system. She'd just never thought they'd resort to violence.

She'd felt for a while like she was being watched,

but Titus' presence may have set off even more alarms.

She knew she should keep her distance from the man.

Yet all she could think about was the fact that he may be going undercover. If he infiltrated this organization, his life would also be in danger.

At this point, it was too late for him to back out.

It was a no-win situation.

Presley paused by Alex's office and knocked on his door.

"Come in," sounded from the other side.

Balancing the box between her hip and arm, Presley opened the door. Her eyes widened when she saw that Titus was still inside.

Both men seemed calm, almost as if they'd been having a pleasant conversation.

More paranoia reared its head.

What if Titus was in on this? What if Alex had sent him to Presley's house as a test of her loyalty?

She'd seen Alex do things like that before and wouldn't put it past him. This whole thing could have been a sham.

But as she glanced at Titus, Presley knew that wasn't the case. He'd always been trustworthy.

Why couldn't she have seen the stark difference between the two men earlier?

Titus stood. "We were just wrapping up."

"Don't leave on my account," Presley told him.

"Let me take that from you." Alex rose from his desk, took the box from her hands, and set it on a table near the window. Then he stepped close, slipping his arm around her waist.

Presley could read Titus well enough to see the flash of discomfort in his gaze. Alex was doing this on purpose. Alex wanted to silently remind Titus that his older brother was better than he was.

Titus nodded toward the door. "I should be going now. But I look forward to seeing you tonight."

"I look forward to that also." Alex straightened, satisfaction glimmering in his gaze as he turned to look at Presley. "You'll join us too, my love?"

Her breath caught as alarm raced through her.

Tonight? What was happening tonight?

Alex's brown eyes studied hers. "We're going to have dinner together."

Her pulse pounded in her ears. That sounded like a *terrible* idea.

But she plastered on a smile and nodded. "Of course. I wouldn't miss it."

"Perfect. Now, would you be a doll and walk my brother out for me? I have some work I need to get done."

As she glanced at Titus, a rumble of nerves rushed through her. "Of course."

The two walked side by side from the office, stopping only to give his information to Alex's secretary. But it wasn't until Titus and Presley were in the elevator that either dared to speak to each other.

"I may have just signed my death warrant," she said quietly.

"What are you talking about?" Titus stole a quick glance at her.

Presley told him about what she'd discovered. About what she'd done.

"Presley . . ." Concern laced his quiet words.

"I didn't know what else to do. I couldn't let anyone use those uniforms. It didn't seem right."

He squeezed her arm in a reassuring manner that made her pulse beat double time.

"I know," he murmured. "I get that. But what if Alex finds out you did it?"

"He might." Presley's spine stiffened. "I think he has someone following me. That same guy from last night maybe."

Titus sucked in a breath but maintained his composure. "Did you see him again?"

"I sensed somebody watching me, but I can't be sure." She quickly turned toward him before the elevator reached the lobby. "Do you know what you're getting into by having dinner with Alex tonight? Are you *sure* that's what you want to do?"

"It's the only way to get more answers."

Before they could talk more, Titus' phone rang. He glanced at the screen before excusing himself and putting the device to his ear.

Based on the sound of his voice, whatever someone said on the other end wasn't good.

The seconds stretched by as Presley waited to hear an update, especially if it related to what was going on here.

Finally, he put his phone away and glanced at her.

"Is everything okay?" she asked.

He shook his head, a new concern in his gaze. "No. That was my team leader. He was calling to let me know authorities just found a dead body in the woods outside of Greensboro. They believe this person was associated with The System."

Titus got ready for dinner at an apartment where Blackout had set up their temporary headquarters.

His own place was only two blocks away from Presley's apartment. His team had set him up there, knowing there was a good chance Alex was watching him. They knew Alex was the type who'd send his men over to check Titus' place while Titus was distracted with other things.

Titus and his team couldn't take any chances.

His mind raced as he combed his hair back.

The man whose body had been found in the woods . . . he'd been a Dagger agent.

Dagger was another security agency, one that took on less-than-savory jobs. In fact, the group had seemed like Blackout's arch nemesis on many occasions.

John McNally had been shot point-blank in the head. But why? And by whom?

This newest development only compounded the fact that The System needed to be stopped. Whatever their goal was, they wouldn't let anyone get in their way.

Not the man who'd been Blackout's first whistleblower.

Not John McNally.

No one.

Though the FBI was keeping an eye on The System, they weren't working fast enough. The feds had to follow certain checks and balances.

Blackout did not.

As soon as Blackout found any useful intel, they'd share that information with their contact in the FBI. But Titus and his team were being paid a pretty penny by Mr. Whitmore's estate to gain this information.

Even if they weren't getting paid, Titus had a feeling he and his teammates would still be on the job. Matters like this were important to them . . . not just as part of their careers, but for their futures as a whole.

Titus glanced in the bathroom mirror one more time, wondering if his brother would approve of his outfit. Alex *always* had something to say about everything. How Titus looked, dressed, acted, spoke. What he did do, what he didn't do, where he went, and where he didn't go.

Alex was a lot like their father—controlling and demeaning. Anthony Armstrong and Alex's mother had divorced when Alex was only one. Anthony had then married Titus' mom, and they'd had Titus five years later.

But their father had always favored Alex, probably because Alex was the man's spitting image and therefore his golden child.

Titus' mom had tried to protect him from his father's harsh judgments and assessments, but Titus knew the truth. He'd heard his father tell his mom once that he hadn't wanted any more children and that being pregnant had ruined her figure.

The two had remained unhappily married until she'd passed from cancer when Titus was sixteen.

As soon as Titus had been old enough to get out of the house, he had. He'd joined the military. His father wasn't a fan of the government or the military. He'd told Titus if he enlisted that he shouldn't bother coming back home.

So he hadn't.

Last Titus heard, his dad had suffered three strokes and was now in an assisted living facility. Sometimes Titus thought about visiting him, but he hadn't been able to bring himself to do it—not after all the heartache his father had put him through.

After Titus finished getting ready, he stepped out of the bathroom and into the living room, where the rest of his team waited.

He'd already given them updates on those police uniforms as well as what Presley had done.

Part of Titus admired her bravery. The other part feared for her.

Based on the gun he'd found in her closet, she'd been thinking about how to escape this situation long before Titus had shown up. Had talking to him given her that extra dose of courage?

If that was the case, he'd be the one to blame if something happened to her.

Which was why Titus couldn't let that happen.

Brandon had set up computers and various equipment on the dining room table, and he leaned over one of the laptops now. Maddox crocheted on the couch while watching a security monitor. Dylan studied some papers in a corner chair.

Brandon stood and glanced Titus over. "Looking good, my friend."

Titus tugged at the collar of his button-up shirt. "Thanks."

Brandon stepped close enough to flick a piece of lint from his shoulder. "You've got this. Just don't show your hand."

Titus appreciated his teammate's reassurance. But his family ties to this case left him uneasy. Still, he *could* do this. He had no other choice.

"How is it going with Presley so far?" Brandon lowered his voice as their gazes locked.

Titus shrugged. "It's had its challenges, to say the least. But I think I'm doing pretty well, all things considered."

"I knew you would. But I also knew this would be difficult. I know how much Presley meant to you."

He and his team had talked about his relationship with Presley before he'd started this assignment. He didn't usually like to talk about matters of the heart, but it had been necessary for this mission.

Titus swallowed hard. "She did mean a lot to me.

But I've moved on."

Brandon narrowed his gaze. "Remember, you need to stay as emotionally unconnected to this as possible."

Emotionally unconnected? He could do that. He'd been trained with the best of the best to set his emotions aside to get the job done.

He nodded. "Of course. No problem."

But the words burned his throat as they left his lips.

Staying emotionally unconnected to Presley felt impossible.

As Titus turned his thoughts away from that subject and grabbed his keys from the breakfast bar, he turned back to his team. "By the way, did you ever find out any more information on that guy that came knocking on Presley's door last night?"

Brandon frowned. "No, we're still trying to track something down. So far, this Jesse guy almost seems like a ghost. But we're doing everything we can."

"I know you are." He let out a long breath and glanced at the door. "Wish me luck."

"You've got more than luck," Brandon said. "You've got skills."

Wasting no more time, Titus left the apartment, ready to get this dinner over with and praying he didn't blow it.

PRESLEY TRIED her best not to look nervous. But to say it was difficult would be an understatement. So much was riding on this dinner, and she couldn't give any signal that she'd talked to Titus earlier.

Though Alex had never said the words outright, it was clear that he believed women should be seen and not heard. Presley was always expected to sit in the background and smile as he schmoozed.

She should be used to it from growing up on the beauty pageant circuit. Everybody had told her she had a pretty face, but that's all they seemed to care about. After some time, she started to believe that being pretty was all she was good for.

Yet Titus had never made her feel that way. When she'd been with him, she'd started to believe in herself. She'd always wanted to get a job in public relations. With his encouragement, she'd applied to a local college and had been accepted.

Then her mom had died, Alex had made his move, and everything had been turned upside down.

She fought a frown.

Instead of dwelling on those thoughts, she looped her hand through Alex's arm as they strolled into Baldwin's Chophouse. The restaurant was housed in a historic, brick-fronted firehouse on the edge of downtown Greensboro. A dress code was required, reservations were a must, and their beef was aged on-site.

Alex loved it here and often made it clear that the restaurant was worthy of his persnickety standards.

Titus waited near the hostess stand when they walked in.

Presley's breath caught when she saw him in his black dress slacks, a sky-blue shirt, and a black tie. He looked like a million bucks, and seeing him dressed up reminded her of the time he'd taken her to a fancy seafood restaurant she'd casually mentioned wanting to go to.

He'd forfeited buying some new rims for his car to take her there—and he hadn't complained once about the sacrifice. He'd insisted that she was worth it—and more.

Alex . . . he could pay for this without blinking an

eye. But had he ever sacrificed anything to make her happy?

She knew the answer—it was a resounding no.

A few minutes later, after perfunctory greetings, they were seated per their reservation at a corner table away from the majority of other diners. The scent of sizzling beef and smoked hickory surrounded them.

Another round of nerves thrummed through Presley as they settled in at their table.

She prayed that this went well.

She knew what was on the line—her life, Titus' life, and probably the lives of other innocent people as well.

After everyone had ordered, Titus turned to his brother.

"It looks like you're doing really well for yourself." Titus tried to both sound cordial and build on his brother's ego. That was usually a surefire way to get into Alex's good graces.

"I definitely can't complain." Alex grabbed Presley's hand and cast a smile at her. "I can't complain at all."

A surge of jealousy rose in him like a monster

trying to claw to the surface. Was that the reaction his brother was trying to get from him?

If Titus had to guess, he'd say yes.

"I'd love to have a lot of chitchat and catch-up time." Alex set his glass of wine on the table. "But there's something I'd like to discuss with you, and I don't want to run out of time."

Titus' pulse quickened. "Of course. You've always been a get-down-to-business kind of guy."

Alex's conniving gaze met Titus'. "I'm looking to hire someone to do some security for me, and it sounds like you might be the perfect candidate."

"It definitely sounds like something I could be interested in." Titus took a sip of his sweet tea. "Tell me more."

"It's for an organization that's just getting off the ground. LifePoint Enterprises. The members are very private and don't like people who ask a lot of questions."

Titus' mind raced. Six weeks ago, a business mogul named Donovan Sullivan had opened a shell corporation called New Life Enterprises. The company had been a cover for a human trafficking organization.

LifePoint Enterprises sounded eerily similar in both name and in structure.

He looked back at his brother. "I can understand

that. I've done many classified missions as a SEAL. Discretion is a must."

The conversation paused as their food was delivered.

Titus wished he could enjoy the savory, peppery steak in front of him. But given the circumstances, that wasn't a real possibility.

"I realize that. However, we don't hire just anyone." A subtle warning drifted through Alex's words.

"What other criteria do you have?" Titus cut into his steak before glancing at his brother, who picked at a baked potato.

"I have to know I can trust you."

"If you can't trust your brother, who can you trust?" Titus' words hung in the air.

He'd asked himself that question many times after Alex had stolen Presley from him. But he hoped his brother didn't hear his sarcasm.

"Exactly. I'm glad we can move past what happened." Alex leaned closer. "So, can I trust you?"

Their gazes locked.

Titus swallowed hard, hoping he didn't show any signs of deceit before he answered.

PRESLEY'S BREATH caught as she waited for Titus to respond.

What would he say?

He knew the stakes.

But Presley also knew that Titus valued honesty. Lying to his brother wouldn't be easy for him—even if the job demanded it.

After a brief pause, Titus nodded affirmatively, no hint of doubt in his gaze. "Of course, you can trust me. I'd be honored to work for you. It would be an answer to prayer, for that matter."

Alex's gaze lit with satisfaction. "Perfect. That's what I wanted to hear. We have a non-disclosure agreement we'll need you to sign."

"Of course."

"I'll have my guys draw it up for you." He

reached across the table. "In the meantime, welcome to the family business."

The family business?

She wouldn't call it that. This was nothing like what Titus stood for. Did he really know what he was getting himself into?

Presley had a hard time believing he did.

She forced a smile as Alex glanced at her. She'd hardly touched her chicken Caesar salad.

She would need to eat if she didn't want to raise suspicions.

Stay below the radar. That was her mantra.

At least, it had been.

She could sense a change coming, however.

"Happy to be a part of it," Titus said.

"Great. I'll pick you up tomorrow so you can work your first day. How does that sound? I know it's a Saturday, but that's when we need you."

"It's no problem. And are you sure you want to pick me up? You don't want me to drive there?"

"No, not yet. I'll need to go over some things with you first." Alex nodded to his plate. "Now, let's eat before our food gets cold."

Presley picked at her salad, her thoughts still racing as the conversation turned toward mutual friends from their childhood and updates on their father's declining health.

Halfway through the meal, Alex's phone buzzed, and he glanced down at it.

His gaze darkened.

Presley's spine stiffened at the look, and she held her breath. She could feel the trouble brewing in the air. "Is everything okay?"

Alex put his phone away and offered a forced smile. "Of course. Just a little business."

Was it the uniforms? Had he seen the stains on them yet?

He hadn't said anything.

But what if he'd put together the fact that Presley was the culprit behind it?

And, if so, what would her punishment be?

Her throat suddenly felt so dry that she nearly choked on a piece of lettuce.

She managed to get a few more bites down before Alex received another text message.

After reading it, he placed his napkin on the table. "I hate to cut this short, but I have some business I need to attend to. Unfortunately, it can't wait."

Her heart thrummed in her ears.

As Alex glanced at her, his gaze traveled to her hands as they rested on the table. Presley's breath caught, and she instinctively wanted to withdraw them and stuff them under her legs—somewhere they wouldn't be seen.

But she couldn't do that.

Everything seemed to go still around her as she waited for whatever he was about to say.

"You need a manicure, my love," Alex said.

Presley released a soft laugh, trying to disguise her nerves. "I guess I do, don't I?"

"Go get one tomorrow morning. I insist."

Her cheeks heated.

Alex knew what she'd done, didn't he?

Was that why he'd brought her nails up?

It was the only thing that made sense.

But what would he do about it?

That was the real question—and the question Presley feared.

Titus wanted to feel victory as he left the restaurant.

But he couldn't.

Not when he remembered Alex's comments about Presley's nails.

Did Alex know what she'd done?

Probably.

And that meant that Presley would have to pay. Maybe not tonight. But sometime.

His shoulder muscles knotted at the thought of it.

Titus understood why Presley had done what she

had. Maybe he even admired it. But she'd put herself in a terrible position.

The good news was that Titus had his foot in the door. He could be close to her. Could keep an eye on things if the situation went south.

He'd start working tomorrow.

However, the job offer had almost seemed too easy. Apprehension rumbled through him at that realization.

Even though they didn't have much time and Titus knew that he needed to work quickly, he'd expected more hoops to jump through before being hired.

His brother had seemed surprisingly pleasant. But he knew that was how Alex worked. He could be charming when he wanted something.

Now The System needed more security?

Was that because they'd killed one of the Dagger agents working for them?

So many questions rushed through his mind as he headed toward the parking garage. He almost didn't know what to think.

When he got in his truck, he'd call his teammates and tell them about this new development.

As he stepped toward his Dodge Ram, a shadow moved behind him.

Titus stiffened.

He hadn't brought his gun with him. It was too risky considering the circumstances.

But his instincts heightened like a fighter jet taking off into battle.

As he glanced behind him, looking for the shadow again, more movement caught his eye.

Another shadow.

Then another.

And another.

Four men in ski masks surrounded Titus in the parking garage.

Each of them had vengeance in their gazes as they pressed closer.

Titus fisted his hands as he braced himself for what could be the fight of his life.

"WE DON'T HAVE to do this, guys . . ." Titus muttered as adrenaline pumped through his muscles.

One of the men—a particularly bulky guy who seemed to be the leader—grunted in response.

Titus considered the phone in his pocket. If only he could call for backup . . . but it was too late for that. He'd have to tap into his fighting skills instead.

He waited, unwilling to throw the first punch.

He'd been in plenty of fights as a kid. He'd learned even more defensive techniques as a SEAL.

But four against one?

Titus didn't like those odds.

Especially because, if he had to guess, these guys were with Dagger. That meant they had just as much training as he did.

Brawny Guy threw the first punch.

Titus ducked.

As he did, another man charged at Titus from behind.

Titus swept his leg behind him, hitting the guy's ankles.

The man fell to the ground with an *umph*.

As Titus popped back onto his feet, the third man charged him.

He tried to move out of the way.

But he couldn't.

Two guys barricaded him from behind, and there was nowhere for him to go.

Brawny drew his arm back, revealing an eagle tattoo on his wrist.

Then he slammed his fist into Titus' gut.

The air left Titus' lungs.

He was trapped now. Unable to use his arms. Unable to get away.

Brawny delivered another punch to Titus' gut, then his jaw.

His head began to spin.

But he was far from defeated.

He raised his legs and propelled his feet into the man's gut.

Brawny grunted again.

Before Titus could make any more moves, the two thugs on either side of him tightened their grips.

"Who do you work for?" Brawny stalked closer, leering in Titus' face with his shoulders bulked with adrenaline.

Viciousness exuded from the man like sweat during a workout.

This meathead lived for stuff like this, didn't he?

"No one." Titus tasted the blood in his mouth but ignored it. He kept his gaze steely instead. "I don't work for anyone. Not yet."

"Why were you talking to Alex Armstrong?"

Titus scowled. "Because he's my brother—not that it's any of your business."

"What does he want you to do?" Brawny demanded.

Titus' mind raced.

Who were these guys?

Did they work for Alex or not?

He wasn't sure—which meant he had to be very careful how he answered.

"I was catching up with my brother," Titus muttered. "That's all."

Brawny socked him in the jaw again.

Pain spread down Titus' neck and up toward his ear.

"Tell us the truth," the man demanded as he towered in front of him.

"I am," Titus growled. "I don't know what you want me to say."

"I want the truth!"

"I'm telling you the truth." Titus clenched his teeth, not liking the position he was in right now.

"Last chance, or I finish you here." Brawny glowered down at Titus, his hands fisted as if prepping for another punch.

Titus braced himself, unsure what was coming next.

Voices in the distance cut through the moment.

People were headed into the parking garage, Titus realized.

The men looked at each other as if recalculating.

Then, one of them pulled something from his pocket.

The men released Titus' arms an instant before electricity spread through his nerves, rendering him immobile.

He dropped to the ground, his legs unable to hold him up.

Then the thugs scattered like birds hearing gunfire.

Presley strolled from the restaurant beside Alex, the sky turning gray as the sun began to sink over the buildings in the distance. Other couples and groups of people were out for the evening, talking and laughing together.

She wished she were laughing as if she didn't have any cares, but her nerves continued to thrum.

What had those text messages Alex received been about?

What had happened?

When the two of them were alone, would Alex unleash his rage on her?

Fear trickled down her spine.

She'd made a mistake earlier with the uniforms.

She rolled her shoulders back. No . . . no, she hadn't.

Presley couldn't let fear dictate her actions.

She'd done the right thing.

Still, she could hardly breathe as she anticipated the fallout.

Alex paused and turned toward her. "Listen, my love. I really need to run."

He gazed at her, something close to tenderness in his eyes.

But it was all manipulation. Presley wanted to relax, but she couldn't.

She kept waiting for the sucker punch—whether it be emotional or physical.

"I don't want to leave you, but . . . I must," he continued.

Momentary relief washed through Presley.

Being away from Alex sounded perfect.

Besides, she'd seen Titus disappear into the parking garage beside her as she and Alex had exited the restaurant.

She needed to talk to him alone, and this could be her opportunity.

"I understand." She squeezed Alex's hand. "My car is right here."

"You sure?" He studied her face, his gaze wavering between concerned and calculated.

She nodded, hoping her gaze didn't show the fear simmering inside her. "Absolutely."

"Thank you, my love. I'll talk to you in the morning, okay? I plan to pick you up so you can come to the meeting also."

"Sounds good." Presley flashed what she hoped was a sweet smile.

Alex watched her as she climbed into her car. But, instead of pulling away, she pulled down her visor and pretended to check her makeup.

Alex hurried toward his car two spaces in front of her, and he drove away.

When he was gone, she scurried from her car and slipped inside the parking garage. A man in all black nearly collided with her as he hurried from the stairs. His gaze briefly met hers before he looked away.

Something about the guy sent a shiver up her spine.

His eyes gleamed with trouble. She'd learned to recognize the look.

As Presley reached the second level of the parking garage, she glanced at the rows of cars and spotted Titus' army-green truck.

She squinted.

Were those . . . legs stretched out on the concrete floor beside the vehicle?

Her breath caught.

No . . .

She rushed toward the figure.

It *was* Titus.

She knelt beside him, soaking in his bloody nose and swollen jaw. No . . .

"Titus?" She shook him, desperate to confirm he was still alive.

He moaned as she shook him again.

How was it even possible that someone had done this to him? He was a former Navy SEAL.

He could handle himself.

There was more to this.

He groaned and tried to push himself up. But he couldn't.

Finally, he muttered, "Taser . . ."

Her breath caught.

Someone had tasered him? Of course.

It was the only reason he'd be immobile like this.

Had Alex sent his men to do this to him?

Presley's blood boiled at the thought of it, and her resentment of Alex only grew stronger.

She'd deal with that later. Right now, Titus was her only concern.

CHAPTER
NINETEEN

TITUS' body either ached with pain or twitched as the zap of electricity slowly faded.

Presley shouldn't be here with him.

It was too risky.

Based on the look in her eyes, he wouldn't be able to convince her to leave. Even in the dim light of the parking garage, her worry was obvious. Everything was quiet around them, signaling those men were gone.

Concern welled in Presley's gaze as she murmured, "Let's get you in your truck."

With some maneuvering, Presley helped him to his feet. He reached into his pocket and used his key fob to unlock his doors.

Presley helped him into the front seat before running to the other side and climbing inside also.

"Do you have a first aid kit?" she asked.

"In the glove box," he muttered, still trying to gather his senses and strength.

She grabbed some supplies and began blotting the cut on his jaw—leaning in entirely too close as she did. Close enough that he could smell her vanilla-laced perfume. Her coconut-scented shampoo.

So close he could feel her body heat—and the shock of electricity that snapped between them. The pulse was nearly as strong as that Taser.

For a moment, Titus felt as if they were cocooned together and the rest of the world had disappeared.

"What happened?" she asked softly as she studied the wounds on his face.

Titus tried not to cringe as the gauze hit his cut. "I think Alex sent some guys after me."

She gasped. "I was afraid of that. Why would he want to hurt you?"

Titus didn't hide his scowl. "I think he wanted to test my loyalty. These guys asked me a lot of questions about what I was up to. I think Alex was trying me to see if I truly could be trusted."

"Oh, Titus . . ." Concern laced Presley's voice—concern that made his pulse beat in double time.

Why did Presley have to sound so sweet? And smell so good? And look so beautiful?

Titus quickly corrected his thoughts.

She was his brother's girlfriend. Titus couldn't think of her as if she weren't—even if the relationship between Presley and Alex was practically a sham.

Until Alex and Presley were no longer together, Presley was off limits.

Besides . . . Presley had already broken Titus' heart once. Why did he feel so eager to give her another chance?

"Should I call the police for you?" Presley stared at his wounds with a frown.

The worry in her gaze was enough to make his heart melt. Titus shook his head, determined to keep his thoughts focused. "No. Absolutely not."

"Your teammates?"

"I'll get in touch with them in a minute." Titus waved a hand in the air, trying to make it seem as if he weren't in as much pain as he actually was. "You've done more than enough. If Alex sees you here with me—"

"He already left. He was in a hurry."

Titus nodded, his head still sore.

"When I first saw you here . . . I thought . . . you were dead." Presley's voice cracked as she slid her hand across his jaw.

He tried not to lean into her touch, to enjoy her closeness. But his body did otherwise.

"You shouldn't be here with me," he murmured, mustering every ounce of his self-control. "It's too risky."

Presley dropped her hand and frowned. "I know. But I feel beside myself. I have no idea how everything is going to turn out, Titus. I'm . . . scared."

He wanted to give her a pat answer, but she deserved more than that. "I don't know how things will turn out either. I just know I need to do everything in my power to prevent whatever it is these guys are planning."

"I want to help you. Just tell me what I need to do."

"I don't know . . ."

"Titus, this is the first time in two years that I actually feel alive again. Everything inside me . . . it's felt dead, like I'm just a shell and all the life has been sucked out of me. I can't live like that anymore. I can't."

Titus stared at her another moment. Part of him wanted to tell her to run. Part of him regretted ever getting her involved at all. Her participation in this put her in the line of fire.

And if something happened to her . . .

He didn't want to think about it.

But it was too late to go back now.

He prayed he knew what he was doing.

Presley wanted more than anything to run her hand across Titus' jaw again. To comfort him.

But she knew she couldn't.

Not while she was dating his brother.

Even if she was only with Alex because he wouldn't let her leave.

Her throat clogged with emotion, and she looked away from Titus.

What was she doing?

If Alex caught her right now . . . she didn't want to think about what he'd do to her, what he would do to Titus.

She had to get a grip. Still . . . there were things she wanted to say. Things she *needed* to say.

"Titus . . . I want you to know . . . when we were together, those were some of the most wonderful times of my life."

His gaze locked on hers, searching for answers. "Then why did you break up with me?"

She glanced at her hands, ashamed of what she'd done. "I'm the only one to blame. But my mother died so suddenly, and, even with our strained relationship, I felt beside myself. I tried to get in contact with you, but I couldn't. You were on a classified mission."

"Go on."

"I called your brother to see if he knew how to get in touch with you. When he heard what happened, he insisted on flying into town." Her voice cracked, and she rubbed her throat, hating how knotted her stomach felt. "I picked him up at the airport, and he took me to dinner so we could talk. After I told him what happened, he said he would help me plan the funeral. That any friend of his brother's was a friend of his."

"How generous." Titus' words sounded dry as he narrowed his eyes.

Presley had to keep her emotions in check for long enough to finish. "Then he started telling me that the nature of your job was that you couldn't be around for major events—like your dad's stroke, for example. You were married to your career; that's what it demanded of you."

Anger flashed in his eyes—but not the same kind of anger Alex showed. Titus knew how to keep his under control, and she didn't fear him.

"As we went through planning the funeral, we kept getting to know each other. As I'm sure you remember, I was living with my mom. After her death, I realized I needed a new place to live, and I was getting panicky about finding a place I could afford. Alex said he could put me up in a place in

Greensboro and give me a job at his law firm. At first, I refused. I didn't want to move away from you. But . . ."

"But what?"

"I didn't realize what he was doing at the time." Shame tinged her voice. "But he kept planting seeds of doubt in my mind about you. About how you weren't reliable. How you weren't the settling down kind of guy. How I'd never have any stability in my life if I stayed with you. At first, I didn't believe him. But Alex was such a rock for me during all of that. So when he kissed me . . ."

Titus' jaw visibly hardened. "He basically convinced you that I was bad for you and that he was better."

"Like I said, it was all my fault. I should have been stronger. I mean, I knew you. I knew you were everything I wanted. But—"

"You don't have to explain anymore. I know how manipulative my brother is."

"I'm so sorry. I've wanted to tell you that for the past two years. But after we broke up . . . you didn't want to speak with me or your brother. You cut us off. So, I couldn't explain and—"

"I'm sorry." Titus' voice sounded soft with surprising sincerity. "I shouldn't have done that. It's just that you were the one thing I looked forward to when I came home. You represented all that was good in the world, and when you were gone . . . I didn't know what to do with myself."

Emotions battered her. Oh, how she wished she could go back and change things.

She'd dreamed about what it would be like to do so.

But that wasn't a possibility, and now she had to live with the consequences of her actions.

She straightened, realizing she'd just opened up an old wound that hadn't healed.

Maybe it *wouldn't* heal.

But she couldn't stay here any longer.

"I should go," she rushed, pulling away as if she'd touched fire.

"Is it safe for you to go back alone?" Titus' gaze searched hers.

So much compassion lingered in his eyes that her heart panged with loss. It had been so long since Alex had shown her even an ounce of sympathy. Any kindness he did show her was just a part of his manipulation to get her to do what he wanted.

"I'll be fine." Her voice cracked. "My car isn't far away."

Before she reached for the door handle, Titus grabbed her hand.

She froze, her heart pounding so loudly she was certain Titus could hear it. "Yes?"

"I'm worried for you. If these guys did this to me . . ."

He didn't have to finish.

Then what would they do to her if Alex felt threatened enough?

"I'm going to put an end to this," she told him.

Titus frowned, though the motion seemed to hurt, before quickly rubbing his jaw and letting out a sigh. "I don't like the sound of that."

"This has gone on for far too long."

"Presley . . . what are you thinking?"

She shrugged and shook her head. She didn't have a plan—only a conviction.

"I don't know," she said. "Whatever it is, it won't be tonight. I need to think this through more. But I can't be a part of this any longer. I have to figure out how to get away."

He squeezed her hand. "I'll do whatever I can to help."

The sincerity in his voice brought tears to her eyes.

She knew Titus meant those words.

Presley had a lot of thinking to do.

But she wouldn't do it here.

She clasped Titus' hand another moment before opening her door and scrambling out. "Be careful."

His gaze met hers. "You too."

But she knew that whatever was about to be set in motion would require risk—and she might not come out on the other side in one piece.

PRESLEY'S MIND raced the next morning.

She knew Alex wanted her to go to the meeting today.

It was Saturday so there was no work. But Saturdays were when The System liked to meet. Instead of making her own plans, Presley waited for his call—to save time she'd already fixed the chipped polish on her fingernail herself rather than getting a professional manicure.

She hoped Alex wouldn't get mad.

She sat down on her couch with some coffee and flipped on the morning news.

As she glanced at the end table, she saw a picture of her and Alex. The image had been snapped while they were at the beach in Miami.

Anyone looking at the photo would think that the

two of them were happy and in love. Their faces almost seemed to be glowing—but that was more because of the angle of the sun than anything she felt inside her.

She'd known after six months of dating that Alex wasn't the man she'd first thought.

She'd tried to leave him the first time after they'd been dating for eight months. She'd told Alex she wanted nothing to do with him and that they were through.

He'd started crying—something Presley hadn't known he was capable of. Alex had begged her for another chance. Told her he would do better.

He'd convinced her he was sincere. Regretfully, Presley had tried to forget her reservations and had agreed to get back together with him.

The second time, she'd had enough—for real this time. Alex had thrown her against the wall, accusing her of making fun of him in front of his colleagues after she'd joked about his Type A personality.

It had been what felt like the final straw. After he'd gone into work the next morning, Presley left without telling him. Fled to a hotel room. She'd even paid cash in hopes of not being found.

But Alex had found her. He hadn't told her how, though she suspected he'd tracked her phone.

This time, he'd been angry.

He'd charged into her room. Before she could react, he'd slapped her.

She'd flown back and hit a table before blacking out.

When she'd awoken, she was in her apartment. Alex had been nursing her back to health as if he hadn't been the one who'd harmed her.

Eventually, he'd insisted that his reaction was her fault. He'd been worried sick wondering what happened to her. All that worry had turned to rage when he'd finally found her. He told Presley she couldn't leave him again and put him through that kind of anguish. He wouldn't tolerate it.

So, she'd stayed with him. She had no choice. Escaping seemed impossible.

But she felt like she'd been living in a prison ever since then.

Her only comfort was in the fact she had her own place. Even though Alex had talked about marriage, he hadn't pushed her to commit. He said he wanted to do things the proper way—when the time was right.

Marrying him was the last thing she wanted to do.

As a news story filled the screen, Presley shifted her thoughts from Alex.

She grabbed the remote to turn up the volume.

A local man had been murdered last night.

Her head spun when the victim's photo appeared on the screen.

He was the man Presley had met at the dry cleaner.

The one who'd given her the police uniforms.

Kenneth.

The truth pounded in her head.

Alex had seen those bleach marks on the uniforms, hadn't he?

And he'd thought Kenneth had done it.

Then Alex had either killed the man himself or he had hired somebody else to do it for him. That had to be what last night's text messages at the restaurant had been about.

Frost spread through her blood at the thought of it.

Titus glanced at his watch as he waited outside his apartment building.

Alex was supposed to be here by now to pick him up. His brother had texted him earlier to get his address.

But he was already ten minutes late, which didn't seem like his brother.

Finally, Titus spotted a black SUV with tinted windows pull up to the curb beside his apartment.

Titus sucked in a deep breath and tried to prepare himself for whatever today would hold. He'd need to be at his best—mentally, physically, and emotionally.

His jaw was still tender, and a small black bruise shaded the skin near his eye from his attack yesterday. His ribs were also sore, but he didn't think any were broken.

His teammates hadn't been happy to hear what had happened, but Titus had insisted he'd be okay. He wanted to proceed with this mission as planned.

Still bracing himself, he watched as the back door opened.

Alex stepped out wearing khakis and an expensive golf shirt and nodded at him. "Sorry I'm late."

Titus resisted a scowl. "You must be losing your touch as you've gotten older. The Alex I remember would never be late."

Alex shrugged and glanced at his expensive watch. "What can I say? Despite all these years when you no doubt thought I was perfect, I'm now proving you wrong."

Titus decided to play off the statement. "What? The entire world just crashed around me. You just admitted that you weren't perfect?"

Part of Titus resented how easygoing and jovial

he'd made himself sound—especially considering he felt anything but.

Alex seemed to buy his act and smiled. "I'm a new man. Presley made me that way."

Titus doubted that.

Alex leaned closer. "Is that a bruise near your eye?"

Titus touched it lightly. "This? Just got into a little scuffle. I'll fill you in on the way."

"Sounds good." He glanced back at the SUV. "Are you ready to go now?"

"I sure am."

"Climb inside then."

Every part of Titus wanted to rebel. His conscience told him not to get inside. To run far from the SUV.

But he was already in too deep.

As soon as they were both in the backseat and had shut the doors, Titus turned to him. He ignored the driver and another man sitting up front as he said, "I think you already know what happened to my eye. You sent those men last night, didn't you?"

Titus had pondered the wisdom in confronting his brother. But Alex knew Titus wasn't the type to let something like that go. That he was smart enough to figure these things out.

"I'm sorry." Alex shrugged, no sign of true

apology in his gaze. "I had to know that you wouldn't talk, no matter what was at stake."

"I guess some things never change."

Alex shrugged again although it looked more like a flinch. "I don't know what to say. It had to happen, though. Consider it an initiation."

Titus touched his jaw as it began throbbing again. "Is this what you do to everyone you hire?"

Alex remained unapologetic as if it weren't a big deal. "Essentially, yes."

Titus' muscles hardened. "And did I pass?"

Alex nodded. "You did. But there is one more thing."

Before Titus could ask what that was, the man in the front seat turned toward him and jerked a black hood over his head.

PRESLEY'S MIND wouldn't stop racing.

She couldn't get that man's image out of her head.

It was her fault Kenneth had died.

She thought *she'd* be the one to pay the consequences, if anyone. But she hadn't considered Kenneth could also be at risk because of her actions.

Sweat spread across her brow, and she wiped it away.

She couldn't show any signs of her nerves—she had to get them under control.

Alex had called about thirty minutes ago and said that he wouldn't be able to pick her up. Instead, he was sending a guy named Duncan to give her a ride to the meeting at the new compound.

The old compound had been raided a couple of weeks ago, and they hadn't wasted any time finding a new hideout. She'd heard that members of The System had upped their security measures at this new location.

Presley didn't like going to these top-secret places. Considering how many high-status people were members of the organization, it surprised her they'd want to meet in such desolate, rundown places. At least, the last compound had been rundown. She didn't know about this new one yet, but she assumed it would be about the same.

Off the beaten path. Inconspicuous. Not a place she wanted to go.

But she also knew better than to argue.

Duncan appeared at her door right on time. Presley had met the man once before, and she didn't like him. Didn't like the way he looked at her. Didn't like the darkness she saw in his eyes.

He looked to be in his mid-thirties, with thinning reddish-blond hair, a slim build, and a disconnected gaze.

"You ready to go?" He jangled some change in his pocket as he asked the question, already impatient although he'd just arrived.

"Of course." Presley grabbed her purse before following him outside to the familiar panel van waiting there.

He ushered her into the back, instructing her to

sit with her back toward the windshield. He then sat beside her. The driver upfront didn't bother to look at her. However, his pungent cologne filled the entire vehicle and nearly sucked the air from her lungs.

Presley never got to see where they were going. Sometimes Alex made her put on headphones, going as far as to test them to make sure Presley couldn't hear anything being said while on the way there.

Would things be different right now if she'd tried to pay more attention? If she hadn't waited so long to be proactive?

Instead of beating herself up, Presley reminded herself that if she'd been too proactive, she could very well be dead right now.

As her nerves tightened, her throat seemed to swell.

"What's the meeting about today?" She turned toward Duncan as they took off down the road. He sat in the seat in front of her, phone in hand and a pensive look in his eyes.

Duncan's cheek flickered as if he were annoyed. "You know I can't tell you that."

"How did you and Alex meet anyway?"

He pressed his lips together before saying, "Through mutual friends."

Presley wanted more details about how they'd

become acquainted. But she knew by the tone of Duncan's voice that he wouldn't offer any.

What else could she ask?

This could be her opportunity, and she didn't want to blow it.

"I can't wait to get to the compound." Presley needed to pretend like she fully supported The System. It was the only way she'd get any answers. "We're doing important work."

Her words seemed to loosen Duncan up, and his shoulders visibly softened. "I agree. This is just what our country needs."

"That's what I keep telling Alex. I want to do more. I'm trying to convince him to let me in on things."

"Well, maybe you can keep working on him."

"I just had the impression that, whatever was going on, it was more of a guy thing, you know? I get so tired of the sexism here. I'm just as capable at helping as anybody."

Duncan shrugged—but the action was more like a twitch. "Alex needs you just to be his soft place to fall. He says that a lot. He doesn't want to get you too involved."

Presley cringed. She could totally hear Alex saying those words. And by soft place to fall he meant his punching bag to relieve stress.

How many people with the organization knew that, though?

She wasn't naive. These people had to know what Alex was capable of. However, he always made sure when he hurt Presley that her wounds weren't visible.

"Do we know when? Do we have a date yet?" Presley stole a glance at Duncan, careful not to sound too eager and raise his suspicions.

He did a double take her way. "You're asking a lot of questions now, aren't you?"

She shrugged. "I'm just curious."

"Then why don't you ask Alex?" he snapped.

"He's been busy lately." She shrugged again, trying to keep things casual.

"Well, I would stay quiet if I were you. Asking questions is a good way to get yourself hurt. Now, if you don't mind, I'd like quiet for the rest of the ride."

Presley pressed her lips together, knowing this conversation was done.

But she still had so much she needed to figure out.

"What do you think you're doing?" Titus demanded as he reached for the hood covering his head.

"Leave it on."

"Why should I?" His heart raced as he wondered what kind of game his brother was playing.

"I'm sorry, but only a few select people can know the exact location we're headed. You're still too much of a liability at this point."

"I didn't prove myself last night when you had your guys jump me?"

"It normally takes someone weeks to prove themselves." Alex's voice remained smooth and unaffected. "But I've had to accelerate things due to some unforeseen circumstances."

Unforeseen circumstances? What did that mean?

Titus drew in a deep breath. "Come on . . . it's me. Titus. Your brother."

"Sorry. It's not personal."

Titus frowned, thankful no one could see his reaction beneath the suffocating hood covering his face.

He should have expected this. Driving right up to this secret location would have been too easy. His brother was too smart for that.

Blackout wanted to put a tail on him today, but Titus had told them it was too risky.

But maybe there was another way he could find out more information. "How far away are we going at least?"

"You'll see." Alex's voice remained unyielding.

"Why is it a secret? I'm going to find out anyway." He didn't bother to hide his annoyance.

"I suppose you're right." He let out a sigh. "We're in for about an hour-long drive."

"Glad it's not any longer. This hood is musty. I hope you washed it in between uses."

"I never took you as a germaphobe." Alex chuckled, clearly loving having the upper hand here.

Alex began going over a list of Titus' job responsibilities. He'd mostly be guarding the gate and checking who was coming and going. Titus shouldn't ask questions. The only people who got inside were the ones on their list.

When they arrived at the compound, Titus would be assigned a weapon and an earpiece. While he was on the clock, they needed his full attention. At the first sign of trouble . . . Titus needed to tell Alex what was going on.

Security was a high priority since they'd developed some enemies over the past several months.

"Do you understand?" Alex asked the question as if he were instructing someone about to take the witness stand in the trial of the century.

Titus leaned against his seat, still processing everything Alex was telling him. "I do."

"What we're doing . . . we don't want anyone to find out."

"Is it . . . illegal or something?"

"Not illegal." Alex's voice hardened. "But we don't want anyone to sabotage our big reveal and ruin our plans."

Titus didn't like the sound of that.

What about Presley? Was she okay? Would she be there?

He couldn't ask those questions, though.

His chest squeezed with emotion as he remembered how he'd felt last night when Presley had leaned close to doctor his wounds. As he remembered her scent. Her soft touch. Her explanation as to how Alex had manipulated her.

He hadn't realized how much he'd missed her, how much their brief time together had meant to him.

Even though Titus had dated since then, no one had ever measured up to Presley.

She's off limits, Titus, he reminded himself.

No doubt this was the first of many times he'd have to repeat that to himself today.

Titus tried to soak in everything he could—even without using his sight or any visuals. The road had turned from smooth to bumpy. The vehicle had slowed as if they were traveling somewhere off the beaten path. Based on the way his body shifted, they were headed uphill. Based on the way the sun hit him, Titus assumed they were headed west.

Finally, they stopped. A window rolled down and wind rushed in. Someone muttered something to someone.

He hated not knowing. Not seeing.

At least, he'd left his cell phone on. Maybe his teammates could ping the location.

Otherwise, Titus would be out here without backup.

A few minutes later, Alex jerked the hood off. The glaring light from the sunny day outside nearly blinded him, but Titus squinted against it.

His brother's smiling face came into view. "Sorry. Necessary evil."

Titus scowled. Alex was enjoying this *too* much.

"One more thing before I lead you to your post." Alex held out his hand. "I'll need your cell phone."

Titus' eyebrows flickered upward. "My cell phone?"

"It's standard procedure. But, just to let you know, as your final test, I'm going to need you to unlock your screen for me so I can read your most recent messages and emails. I have to make sure you're not hiding anything."

PRESLEY HAD DONE as she was asked and remained quiet for the rest of the ride. She'd brought a book with her—a summer beach read that swept her away into a world without any real problems—and she'd tried to read it even though her eyes kept glazing over. Too much was on her mind.

How would she find out more information about what The System was planning before it was too late?

She wasn't sure, but she needed to figure out something soon. All the pain she'd been through . . . it couldn't be in vain. She had to turn this situation around and use it for good.

Titus was the first person who'd ever told her that.

She'd been telling him about how her dad left when she was only a baby. Before they could ever meet, he'd died of a drug overdose. Then she'd been pushed into pageant life and acted as her mother's pawn.

Titus had told her that God could use those awful experiences—maybe to help someone else in a similar place in life. He didn't know exactly. He only knew that there was never a heartache that was wasted.

His words had always stuck with her.

But how was this heartache going to be used for good?

It didn't seem possible.

An hour after leaving her place, the van slowed before stopping. The driver rolled down the window.

A familiar voice drifted into the vehicle. "Good morning."

Wait. Was that . . . Titus?

Presley's heart throbbed harder.

He was already here? Already working?

Presley turned toward Titus, desperate to see a friendly face.

"I'll need to see some ID." Titus sounded all business as he stood outside the van.

The driver held up his ID.

"Who do you have with you?" Titus peered through the window.

"Duncan," the man beside her said.

"And me. Presley Lennox. I should be on the list."

Titus' eyes widened before quickly reversing back into professional mode.

"Presley," he muttered as he looked down at a clipboard. "Yes, you are on the list."

"We good to go?" Impatience tinged Duncan's voice.

"Go on in." Titus stole one last glance at Presley as they pulled through the gates.

Her heart thrummed harder.

With Titus positioned at the compound's entrance, he wouldn't have access to the inside.

She had to figure out a way to find the answers they needed. One way or another.

And somehow, she needed to talk to Titus privately and tell him about Kenneth.

As unseasonably warm heat from the sun trickled through the treetops above, Titus stood in position near the iron gate outside the compound, wearing the black cargo pants and T-shirt he'd been assigned.

Thankfully, he'd passed the phone test with his brother.

Before he'd come today, his team had gotten him a high-quality burner phone with only the minimum installed on it. Titus had added some fake contacts, some temporary social media profiles his team had set up for him, and the device had two months' worth of manipulated cell phone history.

He'd known he couldn't take any chances and that his cell phone could be a dead giveaway.

He hadn't had any time to waste since he'd arrived. Not only had he been assigned a uniform, he'd also gone through some paperwork, including a nondisclosure agreement.

Alex had thought of everything, and Titus had expected nothing less.

Five cars had come through the gate since Titus had come on duty. Another man, Lars, also helped screen the people arriving.

Titus studied the brawny man whenever he could, trying to figure out if this guy was a Dagger agent or if he had some other connection. But Titus couldn't get any information from him.

Lars seemed content to stand with his hands behind his back and stare at the road in front of them as if he were one of the Queen's Guard.

Titus had also noted the eight-foot-high iron fence surrounding the place. They weren't quite in the mountains, but they were close.

The area was secluded, surrounded by nothing but woods.

The compound behind him appeared to consist of a couple of historic buildings, including an old mill and a faded white farmhouse with peeling paint. A small stream flowed beside the buildings, deceivingly peaceful amidst the circumstances.

The whole setup had Titus curious.

He glanced at Lars again, feeling a surge of impatience.

But, as he did, his gaze stopped on the man's wrist.

He had an eagle tattoo.

Lars was one of the men who'd beat him up last night, he realized.

Yet, to watch him now, he showed no signs of recognition or regret.

Titus stored that information away.

Around noon, he spotted Alex and Presley walking toward him hand in hand. Presley was dressed professionally in black slacks, flats, and a pale pink sleeveless blouse.

Another aspect of Alex's influence, no doubt.

She'd told Titus how much she hated dressing up —especially after her pageant days. She'd said she loved being all natural and having a low-maintenance look.

Titus tried not to frown at the change in her appearance.

"How's it going?" Alex paused near him, still gripping Presley's hand—but not in a sweet way. In a way that claimed her as his property.

Titus pulled his gaze up to meet his brother's. "So far, so good."

"Excellent. I have someone coming to relieve you so you can take a break. I've asked Presley if she would show you around. It'll be good for you to get a lay of the land in case of an emergency situation. Plus, you can grab some lunch before going back to work."

"Sounds smart." Titus had been anxious to get a moment alone with Presley all day.

As Alex walked away, Presley nodded toward the old mill in the distance. "Why don't we start over there?"

Titus glanced back at Lars, but the man remained expressionless. Apparently, he could handle the gate by himself for a few minutes.

Titus waited until they were out of earshot from everyone before he said, "That guy doesn't have much personality."

"No, he doesn't. Alex said Lars did a lot of steroids when he was younger and it messed up his brain. But my impression is that he's like a robot, especially when he starts fighting."

Titus had to agree. He'd experienced that first-hand yesterday in the parking garage.

"There's something I need to tell you," Presley whispered as she glanced around.

Titus' lungs tightened. "What's going on?"

"The man I picked up the uniforms from . . . he was murdered."

Titus tried not to flinch at her words, but he was unsure if he'd heard correctly. "What?"

She glanced around again as they walked along the perimeter. "It was on the news this morning. He'd been shot. Do you think Alex killed him?"

Titus' heart pounded harder. He wished he could offer an emphatic "no." But he couldn't do that. Instead, he said, "I hope not. Besides, he's not the type to get his own hands dirty."

"That's what I think too. But he got called away from dinner last night. Remember? He got a message and then suddenly had to go? I bet it was because he needed to take care of that . . . situation." Her jaw twitched as if she fought a frown.

"Did he say anything?"

"No, but I'm thinking about asking him." Presley raised her chin as a flash of stubborn determination filled her gaze.

Alarm raced through Titus when he thought

about that prospect. "I don't think that's a good idea."

"I know I have to be careful. But I'm your best chance to get any answers here. Alex knows what's going on. I need to find out what he knows."

"Presley . . ."

"I'll be careful." She held her head up higher as two women strolled across the lawn close by. "This is the old mill, but we mostly use it for storage."

She spoke loudly enough for anyone close to hear but not to sound unnatural. She couldn't raise anyone's suspicions about what they were talking about.

Once the women passed, she lowered her voice and asked, "Is everything going okay with you so far?"

"Besides having a hood put over my face on my way here today?" His lips flickered down in a frown at the memory. "I guess so."

"They're very protective of their resources here. From what I understand, there's a meeting coming up in an hour. I'm going to see if I can find out what's being said."

Titus stopped in his tracks. "That sounds like a terrible idea."

She turned toward him, her gaze unwavering. "I need to know."

"Presley . . ." He started to reach for her, but he stopped himself. "I don't want you to think I'm pressuring you to do any of this."

"You're not. This is my decision. I'm the best way to find out information."

Titus wanted to argue, but he couldn't. Still, he feared what kind of position he'd put her in. More than anything, he wished he could rewind time.

Too bad he was wishing for the impossible.

AS PRESLEY WALKED Titus back to the gate after their tour and lunch break, her steps slowed.

"What is it?" Titus asked.

She nodded toward the man in the distance. "It's him. The guy who came to my door the other night and asked me if I left my headlights on."

That man *did* work for Alex. She *knew* it!

Titus visibly bristled.

He started to step forward when Presley grabbed his arm. "You know you can't say anything, right?"

Titus stared at the man another moment before his determination seemed to fade, and he nodded. "You're right. I wasn't supposed to see him."

"If you show any signs of recognition, someone might put it together that you were at my apartment." Her pulse raced as she thought about the consequences of that.

Titus nodded again, almost reluctantly. "I'll keep quiet. But I won't like it."

"*You* don't actually need to say anything. I have no choice but to acknowledge that I've seen this man before. I can't pretend that he didn't show up at my door."

Before Titus could stop her, Presley strode up to the man and paused. Her hands went to her hips as her gaze zeroed in on the guard. "I've seen you before, Jesse."

She waited for his reaction, waited to see if he'd acknowledge he'd been at her apartment or if he'd try to play it off.

The man stared at her another moment. He looked basically the same—only this time he wore the same black clothing as Titus and his hair seemed less tousled.

"That's right. I thought you'd left your car lights on. What a small world." The man, with his Texas accent, sounded convincing and slick—which probably made him perfect for this job.

Presley tilted her head. "You didn't know that was my place, huh?"

He let out a rumbling laugh. "I had no idea. But, like I said, I live close by."

Presley wanted to argue with him. To become defensive.

But those things wouldn't help her right now.

Besides, this guy was doing a good job playing off his earlier appearance. If she protested too much . . .

Instead, she cleared her throat. "By the way, this is Titus. He's a new security guard here. Alex asked me to give him a tour and bring him back as soon as he finished lunch."

The two of them had grabbed some turkey sandwiches and chips. Someone had brought enough food to feed an army, and Presley and Titus had eaten their meal on a bench near the old mill.

No one else had been around, so they hadn't been able to overhear any conversations.

That fact had disappointed her—and probably Titus too.

Information was a precious commodity right now.

"Great. I think Lars is going to take a break now." Jesse nodded at the stoic guard on the other side of the gate.

The man snapped out of his statue-like stance and retreated to the farmhouse where the food had been laid out.

As Presley glanced at Jesse, she realized she had

no reason to stay, and she reluctantly took a step back. "I'll let you two get back to work."

But she felt Titus' gaze on her as she walked away.

More than anything, she wanted to stay close to him.

Unfortunately, that wasn't an option.

But she did feel better knowing he was nearby.

Titus had too many things running through his mind as he stood in front of the gate passing time.

Was Presley really going to try to eavesdrop? What would she learn? It didn't matter that Titus had told her she didn't need to do that. She'd do what she wanted either way.

Then he wondered about this other guard standing with him.

Jesse seemed a little more friendly than Lars so maybe Titus could find out information from him. However, Titus instinctively disliked this man, especially knowing that he'd been stationed outside Presley's apartment.

"So, I have an update." Jesse lowered the radio he'd been speaking into. "We have some people coming in a few minutes. We're only checking them by license plate."

Titus stiffened. "Why's that?"

"I don't ask questions. I just do what I'm told."

These had to be high-profile people—people whose faces no one was supposed to see.

That made Titus want to see these people even more.

Just as Jesse finished explaining, a car came up the lane. Titus stared at the luxury sedan with its tinted windows.

Of *course*, the windows were tinted.

There was no way he'd be able to see who was inside.

Jesse grabbed the clipboard from a metal box that had been secured to the gate.

As he did, Titus glanced at the paper there.

License plates were listed.

If he had his phone to take a picture . . . he might be able to figure out who these people were.

Instead, he'd memorize them.

Jesse stared at the license plate of the cream-colored vehicle at the gate and then motioned for the driver to go through.

When the car passed, Titus reached out his hand. "Could I take a look?"

"Sorry. This job was specifically assigned to me."

Jesse shrugged and tucked the clipboard under his arm.

"What's the big deal? I can see the license plates when people pull up."

Jesse remained expressionless, like a good soldier following orders and not asking questions. "I'm just doing what I'm told. Sorry."

Titus frowned and let his gaze wander back toward the car that had just driven through.

The vehicle was already out of sight, parking behind the farmhouse.

Maybe he could take another look before they left and store all the pertinent information about the vehicles away.

Maybe then they would get some answers.

TWENTY-FOUR

"I NEED you to hold the fort down while the rest of us meet upstairs. Understand?"

Presley stared up at Alex as they stood near the front door of the farmhouse. "Of course. Whatever you need."

From the window behind him, she saw another car pull up and park out back. The leadership team was being escorted up a set of back stairs directly to the meeting room located on the second floor. Apparently, that entrance was for *elite* members of The System.

She had a feeling some of the unknown members might be here today. She'd never seen this kind of secrecy before.

Now, she understood. If what Titus had told her

was correct, in only three days something bad would happen.

"It's good to have someone like you here," Alex continued, sounding sweet and caring to anyone who might pass by. "I couldn't do this without you."

Presley swallowed the lump in her throat and nodded. "I'm more than happy to support you however I can."

"Good girl." He kissed her cheek. "I'm really grateful to have you in my life. You make me a better person, Presley."

Even as her stomach turned with disgust, Presley plastered on a smile. She knew she should return the compliment, but the words wouldn't leave her mouth.

Instead, she said, "I'm glad I can help."

"Now, if you'll excuse me, I've got to get upstairs. I don't know how long I'll be. Have fun down here."

As soon as he turned his back, Presley's smile slipped.

Was this what Alex had been preparing her for during the past two years? To be the perfect hostess? To do the behind-the-scenes work so he could attend his secret meetings without any worries?

She'd been trained just like an animal, hadn't she? She'd been programmed not to ask questions or step out of line. As she glanced at the crowd around her, she guessed most of the people here had been through much of the same. They'd been vetted; otherwise, they wouldn't be here.

Twenty or so people were in the room. They were volunteers who'd been recruited to do behind-the-scenes work. Only the chosen could come inside. Even the drivers who'd brought people here were asked to wait out in their cars.

If she had to guess, most of these volunteers, like her, had little to no idea what was really going on. They probably thought these meetings were an effort to develop a third political party to counter the two currently dominating American politics.

Did anyone here know about the danger that edged closer?

She tapped her fork on the side of her glass to get everyone's attention. Remaining composed, she smiled at the crowd as they turned to her.

"We've prepared some food, so please help your-self," she started. "We also have several stations set up. There are lists on the wall. Find your name, and you'll find your task for the day. We have several petitions we need to circulate, as well as new members we need to follow up with. It will be a busy day."

As Presley finished, the murmuring returned.

She knew several people here. She'd made small talk with them during the past two meetings.

But no one caught her eye or raised any red flags. Probably because they were peons, just like her.

Presley somehow needed to figure out a way to get upstairs. To lean close to the door. To overhear what was being planned inside that room.

With the people downstairs focused on their assigned tasks, now was her chance.

Presley glanced around one more time to confirm that everyone was occupied. No one needed her or even noticed her, for that matter.

But once upstairs, if caught she'd need to have an excuse for being there.

She'd already thought it through. She'd stuffed the downstairs toilet with paper until it was clogged and water had spilled onto the floor.

When she'd been helping to set up the room upstairs earlier, she'd seen a linen closet full of old towels. She'd need to grab a couple to clean up the mess.

Quietly, she climbed to the second floor. She knew better than to look around or to give any hints that she was trying to be sneaky. If she did, someone might notice and report her.

Before the first guests had arrived, Presley had explored the farmhouse to become familiar with the layout. Four bedrooms had once been located upstairs. Now, two of the rooms had been converted into one large meeting room. The outside stairway led to a separate entrance to that space.

She spotted the linen closet near one of the doorways leading into the meeting room.

As she grabbed some towels, she would take her time and linger by the closed door as long as necessary. She hoped voices might carry from inside.

A shiver of nerves captured her at the thought.

She walked slowly, nervous that her footsteps would sound on the creaky floor. Muted voices came from the other side of the door.

Presley slowed and glanced around before leaning closer.

No one else was nearby, nor could anyone see her from downstairs. The wall perfectly blocked her location.

As she got closer, a man's voice floated out. "Change is in the air."

Murmuring went around the room as if people were agreeing with him.

"Is everything in place?" This time the voice clearly belonged to Alex.

Presley shuddered when she heard it, the reaction instinctual.

"Everything is in place, and now it's just a matter of time. However, the date has changed. We've moved it up to Monday."

Her breath caught. As Presley clutched the towels closer, the door flung open.

A woman she recognized stepped out.

She'd been caught.

Presley braced herself for whatever would happen next.

CHAPTER
TWENTY-FIVE

TITUS OFFICIALLY HATED this new position. He'd been standing outside this gate for hours, and nothing had happened. Nor was he able to get more information. Nor was he able to keep his eye on Presley.

In fact, he wasn't sure why he was even here.

Neither Jesse nor Lars had opened up to him. This whole undercover assignment seemed to be for nothing except a recap in his heartache.

But all of Titus' grumblings changed ten minutes later when three black sedans came speeding toward the gate.

Jesse muttered something beneath his breath when he saw the vehicles. Then he stepped in front of the entrance, and his hands went to his hips in a protective manner.

"Be ready," Jesse muttered.

What did that mean? "Be ready for what?"

But Jesse didn't answer.

A moment later, a man in a suit stepped out and strode toward them. As he walked, he reached into his pocket and flashed a badge.

"Ethan Murdoch, FBI. I need to speak with the property owner."

"What's the purpose of this visit?" Jesse demanded.

"We're investigating a murder."

Titus' breath caught. A murder? Had he missed something?

Or was Special Agent Murdoch talking about the murder of that guy at the dry cleaner? Had he connected the man with Alex? Or maybe it was John McNally's death.

"I'm not sure what this property has to do with a murder." Jesse's voice remained cool.

"We're investigating what happened and where the crime may have occurred. The body was found farther down river, and this location is one of the few along the path of the stream."

"I'm afraid we can't let you in here without a warrant." Jesse's muscles stiffened, and his voice sounded firm.

The agent peered around them at the buildings in

the distance. "It looks like quite the shindig going on. I need to talk to the owners of this place. A certain LifePoint Enterprises?"

"I can't give you any details," Jesse continued. "You'll have to speak to my boss about that. But I'm sure that he won't speak to you without a warrant."

Agent Murdoch narrowed his eyes. "You do realize that someone has lost their life? A woman. In her twenties. She was brutally murdered, and you could be impeding an investigation."

A woman? Titus tried not to show his surprise.

He'd assumed the murder they were talking about had been that man who'd given Presley the uniform. Or maybe even John McNally. But not a woman.

Jesse crossed his arms, his expression unwavering. "I'm just simply doing my job, sir."

The agent stared at Jesse another moment before offering a curt nod and stepping back. "We'll be back —with a warrant next time."

Titus watched as the agent climbed back into his car. A few turns later, the FBI brigade pulled away, leaving a trail of dust behind them.

Titus turned to Jesse when they were gone. "What was that about?"

Jesse reached for his radio. "I'm not sure. But it doesn't sound good. I know I'm not supposed to interrupt this meeting, but I think they're going to want to know about this."

A dead woman in her twenties brutally murdered and found just downstream from this place?

That did *not* sound like a coincidence to Titus. Not knowing what he did.

Titus feared there might be even more casualties before all of this was over.

He just needed to ensure that Presley wasn't one of them.

"What are you doing up here?" Charlene Moore glared at Presley and quickly shut the door behind her.

Charlene was in her forties, and Presley had never seen the woman smile. In fact, Charlene reminded Presley a bit of an uptight schoolmarm ready to paddle your hand the moment you did something wrong.

Presley had the impression that the woman wasn't an official member of the core group, but that she took notes for them during their meetings. The laptop tucked under her arm seemed to confirm that.

"I had to get towels." Presley held one of them

up. "The toilet downstairs overflowed, and I didn't have anything to clean it up with."

Charlene's gaze narrowed. "You know nobody's allowed upstairs."

"It's just me. I didn't think any harm could come from grabbing some towels. Besides, I can't just leave the bathroom like it is. People need to be able to use it."

Charlene narrowed her eyes even more. "Even so, you know the rules. I'm going to have to report you."

Presley's heart pounded harder. "There's no need. I'm sorry to have upset you. I didn't mean to."

Charlene continued studying Presley, making it clear she assumed the worst about her.

Then her phone buzzed. She glanced at the screen, and alarm spread across her face.

"I've got to go," Charlene muttered.

A sense of urgency seemed to fill the air.

What had just happened?

JESSE LOWERED his phone and turned to Titus. "They're ending the meeting early."

Titus' breath hitched. "The people inside really don't want to be caught, do they?"

"The bigger question is: how did the authorities find out something was going on here?"

His question only confirmed to Titus that whatever these people were planning was shady. Then again, he'd already known that. And the dead woman? That only escalated this to the next level.

"Don't you think the FBI might be waiting at the end of this lane to talk to anyone who's leaving?" Titus asked.

"That's why they're going to leave the back way."

"There's a back way to this place?" Titus hadn't

noticed anything when Presley had shown him around earlier.

"Always have a backup plan. We're going to need to lock these gates, and then we'll get the back entrance opened up. We keep it covered with branches so no one can see it, and the roads aren't on any maps. We need to get everyone out of here before law enforcement comes back with a warrant. Lars is helping with the evacuation."

"None of these guys are going to be arrested for simply being here, are they?" Titus needed to pretend like he didn't know what was going on while still remembering that any normal person would be curious. Besides, working as fake security, he still needed certain details in order to keep people safe.

"Privacy is everything. Each person who's here right now has been assured that their names won't be leaked. If they are, then everything will be ruined."

"Everything? You don't think these people have anything to do with the dead girl, do you?" Titus kept his voice curious instead of accusatory.

Jesse's gaze darkened. "No, of course not. That was just a cover for the FBI to come in here. She was probably a hiker from one of the nearby colleges. It happens a few times every year. People set out not knowing what they're doing, and it ends tragically."

Titus doubted that explanation, but he didn't say

anything. "I don't like the sound of this."

Jesse locked the gate and ushered Titus back. "You didn't tell anybody where you were going today, did you?"

"How could I? Alex had a guy put a hood over my head on the way here, and he took my phone away."

Jesse seemed to think about that fact a moment before nodding. "Right now, you should be grateful for that. Maybe they'll be easy on you for that reason."

But Titus' mind continued to race.

He already saw people leaving the farmhouse. Drivers started their cars and began to line up behind the building. Meanwhile, Lars directed people so everything could remain orderly.

"So, tell me about the road back there," Titus said as he fell into step beside Jesse.

"It's a dirt road so travel is a little rougher. But the road splits three different directions. That way everyone won't come out the same exit and draw attention to themselves."

"You guys really thought of everything, didn't you?"

Jesse twisted his head. "With stakes like this, we had no choice."

Stakes like this?

But Titus knew better than to ask more questions. Instead, he searched the crowd for Presley.

Where was she right now?

And where was Alex, for that matter?

Downstairs again, Presley paced toward the window and glanced out. People from upstairs rushed toward their vehicles in an attempt to get away.

What was happening?

As one of the volunteers scampered toward the back door, Presley grabbed the woman's arm. "Did something happen?"

The woman's eyes darted toward Presley, and she squirmed out of her grasp. "All I know is that the FBI showed up, and we've been given evacuation orders. We've got to get out of here. Now."

Presley's heart pounded harder. Why hadn't Alex told her what was going on?

She took the phone from her pocket and glanced at it.

No messages.

On the positive side, maybe this would distract Charlene from telling Alex that Presley had been upstairs.

Ever since she'd been a part of this, Presley had

never known of the FBI showing up.

How would they have caught wind of what was going on here? Exactly what kind of illegal things could those involved with The System be held accountable for?

If the FBI did raid this place, would Presley go to jail because of her association with the people in the group?

She swallowed hard. She knew the answer was probably yes.

That simply gave her even more motivation to try to find a way out of this.

Next time, she wouldn't let Alex talk her into coming to the meeting with him. The only way she'd participate would be over her dead body.

"Presley," a deep voice called from the stairway.

She turned and spotted Alex heading toward her.

Her heart pounded harder when she saw the urgency in his gaze.

"We need to leave. Now." Alex grabbed her arm and began tugging her toward the back of the farmhouse.

"Right now?" Her pulse pounded in her ears at the near panic that had taken over everyone.

"Yes. We have to leave immediately."

Presley knew she couldn't ask any more questions. Alex took her hand and pulled her outside.

Before he ushered her into an awaiting SUV, she glanced around.

Where was Titus?

Then she spotted him near the back entrance directing people out.

Would he be okay?

She prayed he would be.

A few minutes later, she and Alex headed down the road.

Two other men, as well as the driver, were in the SUV with them, so she knew better than to ask any questions. She'd seen the guys before but didn't know their names. One was a lawyer—she thought. The other seemed to know a lot about state politics.

Tension crackled in the air.

One of the men spoke in low tones to someone on the phone. "That's right. No probable cause. Understand? That's what I thought. Thanks for taking care of this."

What was that about? A case the man was working on?

"Who do you think sold us out?" Lawyer Man turned toward Alex as he shoved his phone back into his pocket.

Alex shook his head, but based on the thickness of his jaw, he wasn't happy right now. "I don't know."

"Could it be your brother?"

Everything went still around her as they waited for Alex's answer.

Presley held her breath, praying Alex didn't implicate Titus. He'd be a dead man if he did.

"Titus had no way to tell anyone where we were." Alex's eyes hardened. "I made sure of that."

Presley released the air from her lungs.

Maybe Titus wasn't on their radar.

Not yet.

But given time, he would be.

Presley had no doubt about that.

Alex turned to her, his gaze assessing her.

Presley's heart thumped against her chest. What was he thinking?

Was he considering the idea that she'd sold them out?

She could hardly breathe at the thought.

If that was where he was going with this, she knew what the end result would be.

Pain and suffering at Alex's hands.

However, Presley didn't think she'd done anything to give him that impression.

She kept her expression neutral.

You haven't done anything wrong.

She had no reason to feel like a suspect.

Presley only hoped that Alex felt the same way.

CHAPTER
TWENTY-SEVEN

AT PRECISELY SIX O'CLOCK, a new guy—someone named Evan Sanderson—showed up, introduced himself as head of security, and told Titus he could leave. Jesse had nodded and acted as if the man was legit.

Everyone else had fled from the compound—everyone but Titus and Jesse. They'd paced the perimeter of the space, waiting for the FBI or any other signs of trouble.

There had been none.

Titus hadn't seen Alex again, not since earlier when he had escorted Presley over to him.

He didn't want to leave. He wanted an excuse to look through things in the farmhouse. But he knew he had no good excuse to stay either.

The good news was that everything was still here. Nothing they'd been keeping here had been moved.

Maybe a team could get here tonight to investigate further.

Instead, Duncan—the man who had been in the back of the panel van with Presley when she'd arrived—drove him back to his apartment with the hood over his head again. Just like the other guards, the man wasn't talkative, and Titus had no luck getting information from him.

But his mind raced.

Titus needed to give his team an update, yet part of him felt like he hadn't learned a lot today.

However, if their sources and intel were correct, there were only three days until whatever The System was planning would be put into motion. Titus didn't have much time to figure this out.

When they'd reached Titus' apartment, Duncan had handed him his phone back and muttered goodbye before quickly pulling away.

After talking to his teammates, Titus jumped in the shower.

Just as he threw some clothes on, a knock sounded at his door.

Who would be here right now? He wasn't expecting anyone, and Blackout knew better than to show up, just in case he was being watched.

He grabbed his gun as he crept toward the door.

When he peered out the peephole, he spotted Presley standing there.

He quickly opened the door. "Presley . . . you shouldn't be here."

"I'm sorry. I had to talk to you."

Titus ushered her inside, quickly checking the hallway to make sure no one was watching.

He saw no one.

He closed and locked the door before turning back to her. "What are you doing here? How did you even know where I lived?"

"You made me memorize your phone number and address—remember?" She sounded breathless as she stared up at him. "I had to talk to you, and I knew it wouldn't be safe to call."

Worry pulsed through him. "I'm not sure it's any safer for you to come here and talk to me."

Titus hurried across the room and closed all the curtains, just in case.

"I wasn't followed." Presley paused near the living room entry.

Titus strode closer as he studied her. "How do you know that?"

"Because I walked here. I took the back way. There was no one. Trust me."

Even the most alert person could be followed

without realizing it. But Titus didn't tell her that now. If Presley had walked here, there was a reason.

"Are you okay?" He studied her face, worried that something had happened to her. Something that he might not be able to see with his eyes but . . .

His gut clenched at the thought—and his fists followed.

"I needed to tell you what I heard today," Presley said. "I knew that there wasn't any time to waste."

His heart thrummed harder. "Okay. Let me get you something to drink."

Presley grabbed his arm before he could slip into the kitchen. "There's no time for that. What I have to tell you . . . you're going to want to know now."

Presley remained where she was—on the edge of the living room—and licked her lips before beginning.

"I was able to go upstairs and overhear a little of the meeting. They've moved the date up. Whatever is happening, it's happening on Monday now."

Titus' eyes widened. "What? Are you sure?"

"I'm sure that's what they said. I wish I could give you more but—"

"You've done more than enough." He touched

her arm, his fingers feather-soft. "I need to make some phone calls. I need to share this with my team."

"Go ahead," she murmured. "If you don't mind, I'll wait."

He grabbed his phone and stepped into the hallway. Presley heard him talking to someone on the other line.

As he did, she paced the living room. She wanted to sit down. To relax. But she knew she couldn't do that.

Too many things were on her mind right now.

After fleeing the compound, Alex had dropped her off at her apartment and said he had some matters to attend to. That's why Presley had assumed it was safe to go out now. Alex would be distracted.

So, she'd put on some leggings, a T-shirt, and tennis shoes and had gone out. That way, if anyone asked any questions, at least she'd have an excuse. She *did* like to jog on occasion. Not as much lately as she did in the past, but the exercise was always a good stress reliever.

Finally, Titus got off the phone and paced back toward her. "My team is on this now. We're going to see what else we can figure out, but knowing the date will help."

She shifted in front of him as her nerves raked

through her in constant ripples of adrenaline. The pressure of this situation was wearing on her.

She pushed a hair behind her ear. "Were you able to learn anything else today?"

"I did get a few license plates, but most of them were rental cars. My guys are trying to track those plates, just in case. But it's clear that whoever is inside those vehicles doesn't want their names to be discovered."

"I'm afraid to find out exactly who is part of this." Presley rubbed her arms, suddenly chilled. "This is much bigger than I ever thought it would be. When these people go down, I'm going down with them."

Titus' expression softened, and he reached forward, gently touching her arm. "I'll do everything possible to prevent that from happening."

Something about the tenderness in his gaze, the concern in his voice, made her heartbeat triple.

Presley shoved aside those thoughts. This wasn't the time to be thinking about her regrets—especially in the romance department. The stakes were far larger right now than her heart.

She swallowed hard as she looked back up at Titus and tried to focus her thoughts. "Everyone is shaken about the FBI showing up."

"I know. I'm afraid it's going to get blamed on me. Except I had no means to contact anybody."

"They're going to search everyone out until they find the mole. Your name was mentioned, but Alex told everyone you couldn't be responsible. He explained all the measures he'd used."

"That's good news, at least." Titus stepped closer, lowering his head to meet her gaze. "The FBI said they found a body downstream. Do you know anything about it?"

"A body?" She gasped. "No. Alex didn't mention anything like that. Whose body?"

"A woman in her twenties. That's all I know. My guys are trying to find out more information about her as well. But the FBI wants to talk to the property owners. That's why they showed up at the compound."

Presley's mind raced. Had she met this woman? Could someone she'd interacted with have been murdered?

She could barely stomach the thought of that.

Every part of her wanted out. Wanted out immediately. But Presley knew that she was in too deep right now—in so deep that swimming back to the safety of dry land wasn't even a possibility.

TWENTY-EIGHT

AS TITUS GAZED AT PRESLEY, he wished she hadn't risked coming to his apartment.

Yet he was so glad to see her.

So glad to have a moment to speak freely without the fear of others listening.

He *had* swept his place for bugs when he'd come in.

He knew it might seem paranoid, but the action was necessary.

It was clear.

As he and Presley stood in front of each other, Titus stared at her another moment. There was so much that he wanted to say—words that pressed on his heart, that burdened his soul, that kept him awake at night.

But she couldn't stay long. She wasn't safe.

"I would love to talk to you more." His throat burned as he said the words. "But we need to get you back."

She nodded quickly, her expression tight and a vague look of disappointment in her gaze. "I know. But I couldn't risk talking to you about this over the phone. I'm always nervous that my calls might be monitored."

"It's probably wise to be cautious. I would get you a burner phone, but knowing Alex, he'd discover it."

Presley frowned. "That's what I thought too."

Titus let out a long breath. "I'm afraid Alex has people watching my place right now too. If anybody sees you leaving here . . ."

"I'll be careful." She raised her chin, but the apprehension in her gaze couldn't be hidden.

"I'm afraid that may not be enough." Titus glanced around again before opening his closet door. "I know this seems very cloak-and-dagger, but how about if we give you a disguise?"

"A disguise?" She raised her eyebrows as if skeptical.

Titus grabbed a sweatshirt. "You could wear this with a baseball cap. I'll put on a hat also and walk with you. When you get back to the apartment, you can slip inside. I don't think these guys will notice you if you're dressed like this when you leave."

Presley stared at him another moment, her gaze pensive. Finally, she nodded and grabbed the sweatshirt, slipping it on. Then she took the hat, shoved her hair inside it, and pulled it on.

The woman was still drop-dead gorgeous. She always had been, and nothing would be able to cover that up.

But it was dark outside, and anyone not watching closely wouldn't recognize Presley in the dim light. The two of them would just need to stay in the shadows.

Titus pulled on his own hat before starting toward the door.

He prayed for the best. "Let's go."

Presley turned to Titus as they paused outside her apartment building's laundry room. She'd fled the building earlier through the small window there and had left it cracked open so she could get back through.

This side of the building was dark, and she'd never seen anyone back here on the small grassy area. It seemed her best bet to use then when sneaking in and out.

Her throat felt dry as she looked up at Titus, only the dim light from the laundry area illuminating his face. "Thank you for all you've done."

"I want you to be careful." Titus reached up and pushed some hair away from her face. He instantly seemed to regret the motion and drew his hand back toward himself.

But Presley craved more. She craved the kind of relationship she and Titus had before Alex had entered the picture.

However, it was too late to undo the past. Whatever happened at the end of this, Presley had to make sure she and Alex were over. Then—and *only then*—could she make plans for the future.

If she lived long enough.

"I'm not sure when we'll see each other again." Presley wished that there was a plan, that she knew what was happening next.

But she didn't.

"I'm sure it will be soon," Titus murmured.

She nodded.

He waved his hand in the air, almost in a half salute as he said goodbye. Presley quickly stripped off the sweatshirt and hat, handed them to Titus, and straightened her hair.

Then she slipped through the window and into her building.

She didn't have to worry about appearing as if she'd just been jogging. The shear stress of the situation had caused perspiration to spread across her forehead. Had tightened her lungs enough that it looked like she was out of breath.

She slipped the key from her pocket and hurried into her apartment.

Once inside, she leaned against the wall a moment, trying to compose herself.

She'd gotten this far, and she hadn't been caught. It probably hadn't been wise going out. But she had to talk to Titus.

She had no other choice.

Presley flipped on the hall light before stepping into her living room. As she did, she saw someone sitting on her couch waiting for her.

CHAPTER
TWENTY-NINE

TITUS HEADED to meet his Blackout team instead of going back to his own apartment. They needed to discuss their next plan of action.

As he walked, he checked his phone for messages.

Alex had sent him a text about an hour ago, but Titus was just now seeing it.

His brother had informed him he would be needed tomorrow and that he'd get further instructions later.

Titus wondered where he'd be going this time.

He'd have to wait to find out.

He unlocked the door at the apartment and slipped inside. His three team members were gathered in the living room discussing something. They all looked up as he walked in, their attention instantly going to him.

"Glad you're here." Brandon tapped his finger on the coffee table. "I made a few calls and found out who the dead woman is."

Titus' breath caught, and he crossed his arms as he paced closer to his colleagues. "Who?"

"Her name was Celeste Davis, and she was a reporter for the *Charlotte Times Dispatch*. Twenty-six years old." A frown flickered at his lips.

"How did she die?"

"She was beaten pretty badly. But I believe the official cause of death was blunt force trauma to the head. Then, whoever did this to her, discarded her body in the river where she drifted downstream."

His lips twitched into a frown. "Someone wanted her to be found, didn't they?"

"I do believe that her death was meant as a statement," Brandon said. "Especially if my theory is correct."

"What theory is that?" Titus straightened.

"I'll let Dylan explain." Brandon nodded toward Dylan.

Dylan lifted his head to address them. "I talked to one of Celeste's best friends. She was pretty shaken by the news. She'd already talked to the local police and the FBI, but she told me that Celeste had been acting strange lately and that she'd been attending some secret meetings that she didn't want to talk about."

"Do you think Celeste infiltrated the group?" Titus' mind raced.

"I'm not sure if she infiltrated it or not." Dylan rubbed his jaw. "I think she was a part of it, but she may have gotten cold feet or even lost faith in the vision. Katie is going to talk to some of Celeste's colleagues to see if she can find out more information."

Katie Logan was Dylan's girlfriend and an award-winning journalist.

"I personally think that either they found out she was undercover or they found out she wanted out and then they killed her," Dylan finished.

Titus ran a hand through his hair as Presley's image flashed through his mind.

That could be her. Presley.

The moment Alex found out Presley was sharing information with Titus, his brother would discard her body in the same way. Well, maybe not Alex himself. But he'd order one of his thugs to do so.

Titus had to make sure that didn't happen.

"There's one other thing." Brandon shifted as he turned toward Titus. "We need to get into that compound."

Titus blanched. "What? You don't even know for sure where it is."

"You said it's an old mill next to a farmhouse about an hour from here. We think we've pinpointed the location."

"That's good news . . ." Titus muttered. "What about the FBI? They said they were getting a warrant to go back."

"The judge denied it, though we don't know why. That said, the best time to go there is at night. You said that there's a back entrance?"

"There is. But my impression is they have security there around the clock."

"Just one security guard?" Brandon clarified.

"I have no idea." He shrugged.

"We can work around that."

Titus' heart thrummed in his ears. He prayed his teammates didn't get caught.

He prayed *he* didn't get caught either.

Because there was no way he was letting his guys go in without him.

Presley's heart pounded into her chest, and her throat tightened until she could hardly breathe.

The figure rose and stepped toward her.

She knew who it was—and that only made her fear swell until it practically consumed her.

"Where were you?" As Alex stepped closer, his face came into view.

Lines formed on his forehead, and his gaze looked dark, ominous almost.

"Alex . . ." Presley pushed a stray hair behind her ear. "I wasn't expecting to see you here."

"I wanted to talk to you. But you didn't answer the door, so I let myself in. I was afraid something had happened."

She let out a shaky laugh. "Something had happened to me? Why would you think that?"

His eyes narrowed. "As you may have heard, a dead woman was found downstream from the compound today. She'd been brutally murdered. I haven't been able to stop thinking about it. Thinking about how someone may be targeting people associated with us."

"Wait . . . was this woman one of us?" Her throat tightened as she waited for his answer.

He nodded solemnly. "Unfortunately, yes. She'd just joined. Someone must have caught wind that she was involved and killed her."

"The people who hate us . . . they hate us that much?"

"Some do. Anyway, I decided I needed to see you

for myself and make sure you were okay."

Presley pressed her hand over her heart. "Alex . . . you're scaring me."

His expression softened. "Don't worry, my love. I'll protect you. But, still . . . having a murder hit so close to home makes you think about things."

"Well, as you can see, I'm fine." She felt *anything* but fine, but she couldn't let him know that.

"Where were you?" Alex's voice hardened again as he studied her like a wolf stalking its prey before an attack.

"Being whisked away from the compound today left me feeling a little tense, so I decided to go out for a jog."

"A jog?" He raised an eyebrow. "You're not generally a jogger."

"My clothes feel a little tight, so I thought I should get some exercise." She figured Alex would approve of her burning some calories. Keeping up appearances was very important to him.

"I think your figure looks just fine as it is." His eyes possessively roamed her up and down.

Presley's throat went dry at the look in his gaze.

She wanted more than anything to step back—but she didn't.

She held her ground.

For now.

"Do you want me to run it past you before I go out again?" The words left a bitter taste in her mouth, but Presley asked anyway.

He stared at her a moment before his shoulders loosened. "Of course not. This just is out of your normal routine, so it concerned me."

Tapping into her best acting skills, she stepped closer and softened her gaze. "Is everything okay, Alex? You've been on edge all day for some reason."

He rubbed his jaw. "It's nothing for you to worry about."

Presley studied him another moment, trying to choose her words carefully. "I saw a news story this morning. The man I picked up your grandfather's uniforms from . . . he's dead. Did you know him?"

His gaze darkened. "Not well. I just hired him to do the work for me. I heard he was one of the best in the area."

"I see. It's just strange. Two murders . . ."

Alex pulled her hand close to his lips. She waited for him to kiss it.

Instead, he studied her fingernails.

Presley's heart pounded so hard she felt certain he might hear it.

He knows, doesn't he?

Alex was thinking about the manicure. The fingernail polish. The drops left on those uniforms.

She barely controlled her tremble as she waited for whatever he'd do next.

Alex pressed a soft kiss on the top of her hand before lowering it. "There's something I want to ask you, Presley."

This was it. This was when Alex would ask her about her betrayal. If she had anything to do with all of this.

If he saw even a trace of deception in her eyes, Presley would pay the price.

Just like the dead girl who had been found in the river.

"PRESLEY . . . I know that we've talked about getting married one day. But I think we should do it now."

Her eyes widened. Certainly, she hadn't heard him correctly. "Now?"

He nodded. "Yes. As soon as possible."

She let out a nervous laugh, trying to watch her reaction—even though her true feelings tried to claw their way to the surface. She couldn't let that happen.

"You don't mean right this very moment or anything." She stared up at him, searching his gaze for the truth.

"Of course not. We wouldn't have time to throw anything together today—or even find someone to officiate it for us. But I pulled some strings down at

City Hall, and I think we should get married on Monday."

Her breath caught.

"Why Monday? Why the rush?" Questions raced through Presley's mind, but she tried not to show her fear—only her shock, which should seem natural whatever her true feelings.

It was one thing to date Alex and feel trapped. But if Presley married him . . . there was no way she'd ever get away.

The thought of waking up beside this man every morning . . . she couldn't handle it. She wanted to physically revolt, but she held herself in check.

Alex rubbed her cheek with his hand, but the motion didn't feel nearly as sweet as it had when Titus did it.

"We've put it off for entirely too long, and I know I've been preoccupied lately with everything going on," he murmured. "But I've realized that's not fair to you. We should make our relationship official. That way I don't have to wonder where you are. You can come live with me."

That meant Alex could keep tabs on her more easily. That he could control her more than he already was.

Then the real truth hit her.

The only reason he'd want to get married quickly

like this was because if she was his wife, then she wouldn't be obligated to testify against him—if it ever came down to that.

He was doing this to protect himself, wasn't he?

More nausea gurgled inside her.

But as she stared up at him, she knew she couldn't say no.

That wasn't even an option.

Instead, Presley plastered on her best smile and said, "Yes. I would love to."

Titus parked the SUV on the edge of a back road leading to the old mill and farmhouse.

He and his team had dressed in all black and were ready to tap into their tactical training. He hoped they could find something here at the property.

They just needed one lead. One break.

Then they'd be able to bring these people down.

Quietly, they headed to the fence at the back of the property. Before breeching it, they paused. Brandon had brought a thermal scanner, and he ran it across the area.

"It looks clear," he muttered.

"No one's here?" That didn't make sense to Titus. Why would the guards leave?

A bad feeling brewed in his gut.

"Let's get in there and do this," Brandon said quietly. "But keep your eyes wide open."

One by one, the Blackout team scaled the fence, remaining quiet as they did so. The sharp wind helped conceal any noises they might make.

The team had already talked through everything on the way here and knew exactly what they needed to do.

They would get into the farmhouse and see if any information had been left.

After Brandon picked the lock to the farmhouse door, Maddox slipped inside and cleared the room. Then the rest of them followed.

Dylan stood lookout near the door to make sure they didn't have any surprise visitors.

The rest of the team split up to search.

Titus bypassed the bathroom, but he didn't see any evidence of Presley's overflowing toilet stunt.

What she'd done had been risky. But considering the fact that she'd heard the date had been moved, maybe it would be worth it.

He headed upstairs to the conference room, each step cautious. His brother was crafty, and Titus couldn't afford to let down his guard now.

The room was empty. Almost as if no one had been there.

Ever.

How was this possible?

Titus would have seen someone emptying the supplies in this area—unless they'd done it all after he left.

He supposed there had been time, but they would have worked quickly.

If members of The System thought the FBI was going to raid the space, they would have taken everything they could. Even after all the key players had left, someone—maybe Jesse or Lars—had probably come in here and swept the place clean.

He frowned at the thought.

If that was the case, where had everything been taken?

"You guys." Dylan's voice came through their comms. "Someone's coming. We need to get out of here."

They slipped outside and headed toward the fence.

Just as they scaled it, an explosion sounded behind them.

CHAPTER
THIRTY-ONE

TITUS WATCHED as the mill went up in flames.

That's where they'd hidden everything, wasn't it?

And they'd set some type of timer so it would explode and destroy any evidence.

But had they put everything in there? Or only the things that were unnecessary?

He'd guess they took some of the supplies with them when they'd fled. It only made sense.

His heart pounded harder.

On one hand, he was thankful that none of his team had been inside.

On the other hand, he wished they'd had a chance to check it out. To take pictures—to find *something*.

"Come on," Brandon muttered. "We need to get out of here before fire and rescue come."

With one last glance, he climbed back into the SUV and they took off down the road.

"I found something." Maddox held up a paper in his hands. "It was under a rug. I don't think anyone meant to leave it behind."

"What is it?" Titus asked, keeping his eyes on the road.

"A flyer for a campaign rally for Senator Erwin Gately," Maddox said.

Senator Gately had nearly been assassinated in front of the North Carolina State Capitol a few weeks back. The bullet had hit his shoulder, but thankfully he was recovering.

"Are these guys still targeting Senator Gately?" Titus muttered. "Why him of all people?"

"Maybe these guys are targeting his campaign rally. Look at the date." Brandon pointed to some numbers on the flyer. "It's now taking place on Monday, though it was originally scheduled for Tuesday. It matches."

"So, these guys are targeting Senator Gately again," Maddox said with a grunt. "They're going to strike at his rally. We have to warn him—and tell the FBI."

Senator Gately didn't seem the type to raise any red flags. He wasn't particularly divisive. He had good poll numbers. His community loved him.

Why target him of all people? Why not the speaker of the house? The head of the arms committee?

As far as Titus knew, Gately didn't hold any positions of power within the Senate—other than simply being a senator.

"I agree," Dylan said. "If his life is on the line, we have a moral obligation to tell him what's going on."

"I'll do that," Brandon said. "We don't have any time to waste."

As they headed down the dark, wooded road, the compound disappeared from sight behind them.

If Titus had to guess, these guys wouldn't be coming back here.

His team would need to think of another way to get information.

But the sooner this was over, the sooner he could whisk Presley away from here.

Even though it was almost two a.m., Presley couldn't sleep.

She had too much on her mind, and time wasn't on her side.

So, she got dressed, sneaked outside, and found a payphone—one of the few left in the city. But she'd passed by it several times before and knew it was there—and knew it was perfect for making a discrete phone call.

She called Titus. She hoped she didn't wake him, but she thought he'd understand if she did.

Presley knew it was risky, but she had no other choice.

She wasn't sure about anything except for the fact she needed to talk to him.

He answered on the first ring. "Hello?"

"Titus. It's me."

"Presley?" Alarm shot through his voice. "What's wrong?"

"I have to talk to you. Now."

"Okay. What's going on?"

"No, not on the phone. In person." She glanced around the sidewalk, halfway expecting someone to step from the shadows again.

She was shaken after Alex's visit, to say the least.

"Presley, you're worrying me." Concern crackled his voice.

She drew in a shaky breath. "It's important. I wouldn't have called if it wasn't."

Titus paused but only for a few seconds. "Okay. We can meet. But you're going to need to listen closely to my instructions."

Presley took mental notes as he rattled off his plan.

She ended the call and slipped into the shadows to wait.

Her whole body was on edge. Her nerves thrummed. Her throat felt tight. Even her jaw hurt, a reminder not to clench her teeth.

She didn't think anyone had followed her. But that didn't stop her body from jerking at every unexpected sound.

Five minutes later, a vehicle rounded the corner and pulled up beside her.

Titus had said he'd meet her out here. But this wasn't the truck she'd seen him driving before.

Had one of Alex's guards found her?

Her heart beat harder.

She tensed. Ready to flee.

But when the window rolled down, Titus stared back at her.

Relief flooded through her. Quickly, she jumped inside, and he took off.

"Whose car is this?" Presley glanced around. "I was expecting to see your truck."

"Sorry if I scared you. It belongs to a teammate," he told her. "I was afraid Alex might be tracking my truck."

"Good thinking." She rubbed her arms, suddenly chilled.

"Why did you need to meet with me in the middle of the night? What's going on?"

"Is there anywhere you could pull over?"

A few minutes later, he pulled into a church parking lot and backed up against the building. From here, he could see anyone coming and going.

Then Titus turned to her. "Now, you've got to tell me what's wrong before my mind goes crazy with worst-case scenarios."

CHAPTER
THIRTY-TWO

TITUS' thoughts wouldn't stop racing. Ever since he'd heard the panic in Presley's voice, he knew that something was wrong.

If she'd risked so much to call him, that fact only confirmed his suspicions. However, he worried about the consequences of that one act.

What had happened in the three hours since they last talked?

Tears streamed down her face as she turned to him. "I'm sorry to drag you into this."

"If I remember correctly, *I'm* the one who dragged *you* into this."

She wiped her cheeks with the back of her hands. He wished he had something to offer her, but he didn't.

"When I got back to the apartment tonight, Alex was waiting for me."

Titus' eyes widened. "Did he know that we were together?"

She shook her head. "I don't think so. It was even worse than that."

"What do you mean? Did he hurt you?" His pulse pounded at his temples as he waited for her to continue.

"Oh, Titus . . . he said he wants to marry me."

His shoulders softened just slightly. "I'm sure he's probably said that before, hasn't he?"

"In two days. He said we need to get married in two days. And I know I cannot tell him no."

The pounding at his temples grew stronger, louder.

If Presley married his brother . . . then she'd *definitely* be off-limits.

"Presley . . ."

As he said her name, she leaned toward him and fell into his arms. Instinctively, he tightened his hold on her and pulled her close, wishing there wasn't a console separating them.

He held her as she wept. He wished there was something he could tell her, but there wasn't.

The only thing he knew for certain was that he

cared about this woman. Despite the history between them, Titus' feelings had never died.

Sure, he had been angry. But once he'd moved past that, he'd remembered what an amazing woman Presley was.

And the fact that his brother was abusing and manipulating her only made Titus irate.

As Presley drew her head back, their eyes caught. His gaze went to her lips.

He'd love nothing more than to recreate some of the kisses they'd shared back when they were dating.

Titus could tell by the look in her eyes that she wanted it too.

His throat felt as dry as a desert as he weighed his options. Follow his heart? Follow logic?

He knew what he wanted to do.

But he had to be wise. He couldn't be like his brother—even if the war raging inside him made him feel as if he was being torn apart.

"I . . . I can't." He sat back and raked a hand through his hair. Letting go of her, his entire body felt as if it had come unplugged and resulted in a citywide blackout.

Presley lowered her lids and crossed her arms over her chest. "Of course."

"It's not that I don't want to," he rushed. "But as long as you're dating my brother . . . I vowed that I would never be that type of guy. I won't cheat. And I won't be with someone who's cheating."

"I can respect that. I think the moment just got the best of me."

"Presley . . ." He licked his lips. "I could help you leave him."

"I thought about that. And it's tempting. But I need to stay until this is all over."

"There's something I need to tell you . . ."

Her eyes widened. "What's going on?"

"My guys and I . . . we snuck into the compound tonight. I'd just gotten back to my apartment a few minutes before you called."

Her eyes widened even more. "What?"

"No one caught us. But the place was wiped clean. There was no evidence of anything—what the meeting was about, any supplies they needed for what they were planning. Nothing."

"Really?"

"Really. Right before we left, the old mill exploded. I'm assuming everything was inside."

"Everything? You think all the evidence of what they've been doing has been destroyed?"

Titus let out a breath. "Maybe not. Do you know of any other place they might have taken at least a portion of their supplies?"

Her gaze wavered back and forth before she

finally shook her head. "No. I don't know. I mean . . . they're all too smart to take them to their homes."

"I agree. But we need to figure out where they've stored them. We're running out of time. The only thing we found was a flyer for a rally for Senator Gately. It's taking place on Monday."

Fear flashed through her eyes before she quickly nodded. "I'll see what I can do."

He frowned as he gazed at her. "I don't want you to put yourself in any dangerous situations."

"I won't."

Their eyes locked as certainty consumed his gaze. "And I'll think of a way to prevent that wedding from happening. I promise."

Presley stared at him another moment, more moisture filling her gaze. "Thank you."

Titus let out a shaky breath. "I should probably get you back now, though."

She wiped her eyes one more time. "It's probably a good idea."

But another part of him was disappointed. He didn't want to drop her off. Didn't want to leave her. Didn't want things to be this way.

But they couldn't change their circumstances.

Not yet, at least.

Presley hurried back toward her apartment building after Titus dropped her off, her heart racing out of control.

He'd wanted to kiss her. She'd seen the desire in his gaze.

And Presley wanted to kiss him too. More than anything.

But Titus was right to stop it. Even if her relationship with Alex was a sham, that still wouldn't be the right thing to do.

But being this close to Titus and not being able to rekindle their old relationship . . . it made her heart feel shattered.

As she reached the parking lot, she stared at the entrance to her apartment building.

She couldn't go back inside. It didn't matter that it was late. The middle of the night, for that matter.

She wasn't tired. She couldn't allow herself to be tired. Not when so much was on the line.

And while she was still alert, she should find answers.

Decision made, she reached into her pocket and pulled out her car keys. Then she hurried to her sedan, praying no one was watching.

Where would Alex and his friends have left those bomb-making materials?

Presley had been telling the truth when she'd said

these guys were too smart to take anything like that into their homes. Nor would they trust just anyone else to keep the supplies for them.

They could have some other property she didn't know about. But Presley didn't think that was the case. Before they'd gained ownership of this current property, she'd heard murmurings about the deal. She hadn't heard talk about any other properties, however.

But there was one place she could think of. Last year, Alex had taken her for a weekend trip to a cabin located in the foothills. It was owned by a friend of his who said he could come and go whenever he wanted. In fact, this friend and his family had moved to California not long ago, so Presley knew that the place should be empty.

She could call Titus and ask him to go with her. But she'd already put him at risk too many times.

No, she'd simply go check it out, and, if there was anything to report, she would call him.

First, she wanted to see the place for herself.

She hoped she didn't regret it.

But her adrenaline was pumping too hard for her to go to bed anyway. So, she might as well do something useful with her time.

She plugged in the approximate location on her

GPS. If she could get to the basic area, she felt certain she could find the cabin.

The location was fifty miles away.

Presley took off down the road, her thoughts racing along with her car.

PRESLEY'S THOUGHTS raced the entire drive. But she hadn't changed her mind. This was what she needed to do.

Finally, after driving through what seemed like absolutely nothing for the past twenty minutes, she was almost at the location.

Just to be certain, she couldn't pull up to the house. It was too risky. Especially in case somebody was there.

Instead, she drove past the place.

The cabin looked dark, with no cars in the driveway. A lone light poured illumination on the gravel drive out front, probably a security measure.

Presley parked down the road at an empty house. Then she hiked through the woods until she reached the cabin.

The place was set back from the road and would be the perfect place to hide something.

She climbed up the back steps, her gaze darting around as she did just to make sure no one else was here.

When she got to the back door, she reached beneath the welcome mat and found the key. She remembered that was where it was kept from when Alex had brought her here.

As quietly as possible, she slid it into the lock and twisted.

The handle released when she opened the door, and she pocketed the key before quietly slipping inside.

Darkness waited for her.

She didn't dare turn on any lights. Instead, she used the light on her cell phone to guide her way.

She shined the beam around the space, but nothing caught her eye.

From what she remembered, there were at least six boxes of supplies. It would be hard to miss them. It was too much to leave in a regular-sized closet.

So where would somebody put them if they wanted to keep them out of sight?

Was there any proof someone had even been here since they fled from the compound earlier?

Presley studied everything around her, but she

didn't see any signs that anyone had been here recently.

Yet that didn't mean they hadn't.

She moved from the kitchen to the dining room and living room.

There was nothing.

She searched the first bedroom she came to.

It was clear.

So was the second.

As she stepped into the primary bedroom, her flashlight stopped on some dirt on the floor.

The small clumps looked fresh. Damp. Not dried and old.

Her breath caught.

Someone had been in here.

She quickly scanned her surroundings, looking for those supplies.

But they weren't out in the open. These guys were too smart for that.

She glanced at the closet.

Was this it? Were they in there?

She didn't think the materials could all fit inside, but maybe Alex's guys had managed to get them in there somehow.

Before she could open the door, headlights grazed the window.

The headlights of someone turning into this driveway.

Panic seized her lungs until she couldn't breathe.

Who was here?

It didn't matter.

All that mattered right now was that she hid.

Titus put his phone to his ear as he stepped into his apartment.

He recognized the number calling him as belonging to Thomas Williams, a new guy who'd just come to work for Blackout a couple of weeks ago. He wasn't special forces, but he was helping them with surveillance when needed.

He'd been keeping an eye on Presley.

"She left," Thomas rushed.

Titus froze in his entryway. "What do you mean?"

"When Presley came back from meeting with you, she hopped in her car and went somewhere. I followed her, but my tire hit a pothole and it popped. Last I saw her she was heading toward an intersection." He gave Titus the street names.

"Thanks for trying." As Titus ended the call, his muscles stiffened.

He'd assigned Thomas to keep tabs on Presley.

Especially now that he knew what was going on, Titus knew she needed an added layer of protection. He would have done it himself except he needed some rest so he could be at his best during the day.

The same went for the rest of his team. They needed to be ready for whatever might happen on Monday. That's why he'd asked for Thomas.

But now he could see that had been a mistake.

Where was Presley going?

Instead of settling in at his apartment, he stepped back outside.

He needed to find her.

Titus had even considered putting a tracking device on her car or in her purse. But that seemed like such an invasion of privacy.

Or like something that Alex would do.

So, Titus hadn't. But now that felt like a mistake too.

What if Presley was in danger?

Or what if she'd figured out where they'd taken those bomb-building materials and she'd gone to look for herself? Wouldn't Presley have asked him to go with her?

Titus would like to believe she would, but she might believe she'd already put him at risk too many times. Knowing Presley, that was precisely what she would think.

And that wasn't okay. Titus had to find her before Alex did.

He wanted to call her or text her, but he felt certain that Alex was monitoring that phone. So, what else could he do?

Thomas had said he had lost Presley near an intersection. Titus would go there first. Try to put himself in her shoes.

It was a long shot, but he had to do *something*.

In the meantime, he called Blackout's tech guy and asked him to see if he could get a trace on her phone.

Titus couldn't lose Presley again before he had a fighting chance of winning her back.

But the situation they were both in . . . it was dangerous, to say the least.

THIRTY-FOUR

PRESLEY barely fit under the bed. There was probably only an eight-inch clearance. But she'd managed to squeeze herself between the bed and the floor, and now she lay with dust balls and dried leaves and who knew what else.

But she didn't care right now.

Not really, at least.

What she cared about was making herself small. Making sure that whoever was here wouldn't find her.

Her heart thumped against her ribcage so loudly that she felt like it vibrated the floor. But that was a crazy thought. Of course, that wasn't going to happen.

The headlights out front cut off.

A moment later, the wooden porch steps groaned under the weight of the visitor.

Keys jangled, and the door opened.

Whoever was here also had a key. But Presley wasn't sure how many keys had been given out to this place.

Footsteps pounded across the floor. The living room.

Then closer.

In the hallway. That's how it sounded.

Please, don't come in here. Please. Presley silently prayed the prayer.

But she knew it was too late.

Whoever was here was *definitely* coming into this room.

She was nearly certain those supplies were now in this closet.

As the door to the room opened, she dug her fingers into the wooden floor beneath her. She pressed her eyes shut, trying to pretend she wasn't here. Silently reminding herself not to make any movements.

She could hardly even breathe, afraid the mere act of doing so would somehow draw attention to her.

Whoever had entered turned on the light.

She expected the person to walk directly to the closet.

But, instead, he walked toward the bed.

Her eyes popped open as she waited. As she anticipated.

At any moment, she expected to see a face drop down and stare at her.

Someone knew she was here, didn't they?

Did the house have an alarm?

Or had a camera been set up so someone saw her come in?

Instead, shoes came into view as the person stood directly in front of her, facing the bed.

Did he have a gun? Would he simply aim it at the mattress and shoot through it until a bullet reached her?

She couldn't be sure.

But even through the darkness, she thought for sure she knew who those shoes belonged to.

Alex.

She was almost certain that Alex was the one who was here.

Titus continued down the road, keeping his eyes open as he searched for any sign of Presley. Why would she have left again? And without telling him?

He didn't know. But all he cared about right now was finding her and knowing that she was safe.

The thought of her marrying Alex . . . it did something strange to his heart. He couldn't let that happen. One way or another, he had to stop it.

The roads around him became darker and narrower. Was this the way Presley had come? There were only two directions she could have turned after Thomas' tire had blown.

Titus tried to put himself into her head.

His white knuckles formed peaks as he gripped the steering wheel even harder.

One of his mentors always said that things had a way of working out the way they were supposed to. Titus tried to believe that.

But now he wasn't sure that he could.

He didn't see how this situation could work out in a good way. In fact, everything seemed to be heading in the opposite trajectory.

A road appeared on his left, and he glanced that way. Though this felt like a wild goose chase, there was no way he was going back to his apartment and just sitting there. So he might as well drive.

He turned down the road and continued to scan everything around him.

Bigger homes were located out here—homes with more acreage for those who didn't like life in the city or the suburbs. The landscape became hilly as he traveled toward the mountains.

Somewhere out here, he thought he remembered hearing about a lake with some vacation houses. One of Alex's high school friends had talked about going there once—going to a house on Loch Ness Lane. The name was nearly unforgettable.

Loch Ness Lane?

Was there any chance Presley could have headed there? It was in this general direction, and Alex had been friends with the family who owned it.

Titus turned over that possibility as he headed down the road.

Even if that was where she'd gone, where exactly was that cabin?

Titus never thought he'd be back in this area, or he would have paid more attention to the details of those past conversations. He was officially headquartered out of Lantern Beach right now. But this assignment had pulled him back into his past—a place he'd rather not be.

He stared straight ahead, hoping for a glimpse of Presley's car or a sign of where to go.

The road in front of him was empty.

Discouragement blasted him like a man facing a firing squad.

He could be headed in the totally wrong direction.

On a whim, he typed Loch Ness Lane into his GPS.

Sure enough, the road popped up. It was only ten minutes away.

Since it was out here, it was worth a shot.

As soon as he reached the quiet, lonely road, he began scanning the driveways he passed, looking for any type of clue.

His foot hit the brakes when he saw a car parked near a cabin.

The license plate on the car, illuminated by a small overhead light, caught his eye.

SHARK.

His brother was there.

Titus' heart pounded harder.

Was this where Presley had gone?

His mind raced.

As he continued down the road, a familiar car caught his eye.

Presley's.

It was parked in the driveway leading to a dark house.

The vehicle appeared to be empty.

He needed to get to the bottom of whatever was happening.

CHAPTER
THIRTY-FIVE

PRESLEY'S HEART continued to beat in her ears.

She stared at the feet in front of her.

She was certain it was Alex. And he had paused right there.

Maybe he wanted to draw this out. To torture her. To make her anxiety skyrocket as she waited for whatever would happen next.

But all she knew was that she needed to be absolutely still.

If by any chance he didn't know she was here, she needed to keep it that way.

Her fingers dug deeper into the wood floor. She should have never come here. What had she been thinking?

Alex turned, his shoes now facing toward the door.

What was he doing? Did he know something was wrong in here? Her feet weren't hanging out the side of the bed or anything, were they? Or had she left an impression in the dust on the floor by the bed?

He was a detail person, the kind of guy who picked up on nuances like that.

She should have thought this through better.

She should have hidden somewhere else. In the bathroom maybe.

But she knew nowhere was safe right now.

As the dust around her shifted, she felt a tingle in her nose.

No, not now. She couldn't sneeze, whatever she did.

But the dust continued to cause her nose to twitch.

She pressed her eyes closed and prayed.

No, no, no . . .

The feeling went away.

But she knew that it probably wasn't permanent.

Just then, her phone rang.

Her heart lurched into her throat.

Until she realized that it wasn't her phone.

Hers was on silent.

Instead, it was Alex's.

"What's going on?" His deep voice filled the room as he paced away from the bed.

Some of the air left her lungs—but not too much. She was still in danger.

"Right," he said. "I understand. It sounds like everything's moving forward according to plan. You have the speakers ready?"

The speakers? Who was speaking and where?

What he said didn't make any sense. She knew that The System was planning some type of event . . . some type of Great Awakening. But she had no idea about any of the details.

"That sounds perfect," Alex said before pausing. Then, "Yes, that's been taken care of. He shouldn't give us any more problems."

Taken care of? Any more problems?

Cold fear spread down her spine.

Who was he talking about?

A moment later, the closet door opened. Alex grunted as if lifting something.

Then the bedroom light cut off as his footsteps left the room.

She listened as the door opened and closed. Then the car started and pulled away.

It appeared that Alex had left.

But that had seemed too close for comfort.

Titus cut his headlights as he headed back down the road toward the cabin where he had seen Alex's car.

Just as he rounded the bend, he saw a vehicle pulling out of the driveway and heading in the opposite direction.

He tapped his brakes and waited until the car disappeared from sight.

When he was sure that Alex was gone, he pulled into the driveway, his headlights still off.

He couldn't be sure that no one else was inside this place even though he didn't see any cars. And he couldn't be sure that Presley wasn't with Alex in that vehicle.

Had they secretly met here?

He had no idea.

But he wanted to find out.

Moving quietly, he went around to the back door. He tried the handle and discovered it was unlocked.

Unlocked? That was surprising.

As he opened it, he scanned everything inside, looking for any sign that someone might be here.

But he saw nothing.

And just to be certain, he pulled the gun from his holster.

He didn't trust his brother. And Titus didn't know if he was walking into some type of trap.

Remaining on the edge of the wall, he crept across

the space, looking for any signs of danger—or a clue as to what his brother might have been doing here.

Just as he reached the corner leading into the hall-way, he heard a sound.

Someone else *was* here.

He couldn't chance being caught.

He slipped into the shadows and waited for the figure to emerge.

PRESLEY WOULD EXIT the way that she had come.

Through the back door.

She stayed quiet, just in case.

Even though she'd heard Alex leave, she still had to be careful.

But all she wanted right now was to get back inside her apartment and lock the door.

She needed to feel safe—although, if she were honest with herself, she hadn't felt safe in a very long time.

Just as she turned toward the kitchen, she glanced to her side.

A figure stood there holding a gun.

She stifled a scream as she scrambled back.

Then she realized who it was.

"Titus?"

He stepped closer, lowering his gun. "Presley?"

"What are you doing here?" They both asked at the same time.

"I remembered that I'd come to this place with Alex before, and I wanted to see if this might be where he brought their supplies," she explained.

"I had a guy stationed outside your apartment, on the lookout for trouble. He saw you leave and followed you, but he blew a tire. I got worried, and I decided I would drive all night if I had to if that's what it took to find you."

"Oh, Titus . . ." She rested her hand on his chest—but only for a moment. Then she quickly pulled her arm back as if she'd touched fire.

She couldn't let herself go there.

His jaw tightened, and Presley knew he wanted to hold her also.

But they both knew the stakes here.

It was too soon. Too much was on the line.

Titus cleared his throat. "Did Alex catch you?"

"No, I thought he was going to. I thought he may have even followed me. But I don't think he knew I was here. However, someone called him while he was inside, and Alex mentioned that someone had been taken care of."

"What's that mean?"

She shrugged. "I don't know. I was afraid he was talking about you. He also said something about speakers."

"Speakers?"

She shrugged. "I don't know what they're planning. Sometimes they'll protest different campaign rallies, and Senator Gately has one coming up."

"That would make sense."

"They have to be planning something for that rally. It's the only thing that makes sense. I checked the closet, but it's empty. I thought for sure they'd brought everything here. Alex did take something from it, but I couldn't see what it was."

Titus leaned closer. "You should run, Presley."

"I can't . . ." Her voice cracked.

"I can help you. I'll make sure Alex never finds you again."

She shook her head, wiping at the moisture beneath her eyes. "I know . . . but I can't leave yet because you guys still need me. I can't walk away from this."

"But . . ."

She knew why he couldn't finish his statement.

Because if she didn't walk away now, there was a good chance she wouldn't come out of this alive.

She ran her hand down Titus' cheek. "Everything will be okay."

Titus swallowed hard, looking as if he fought his own emotions.

Finally, he nodded. "You should get back before Alex somehow notices that you're gone."

After Titus had tracked down Presley last night, he followed her back to her apartment and waited until she was safely inside before leaving. Just as before, Thomas kept watch outside her apartment, just in case. Blackout had given him a new vehicle until his tire was fixed.

Titus could feel the noose squeezing tighter.

Whatever was happening, it was becoming all too real. The stakes were entirely too high. Not only that, but time was running out.

Titus' phone rang at 6:30—while he was still in bed.

Thankfully, he wasn't the sleeping-in type.

On the other hand, it didn't really matter since he'd hardly gotten any rest last night.

It was Alex.

"Good morning, Titus. I was wondering if I could stop by. I have a couple of things to talk to you about."

Titus' heart pounded harder in his ears as he

pushed himself up in bed. He didn't like the sound of that. But he had to play it cool.

"Of course. When do you want to come over?"

"I'm actually outside."

Titus' eyes flickered up. "Outside my place? Right now?"

"Yes."

"I'll be right there."

Titus threw some clothes on and then started to the door. Sure enough, Alex stood outside with two cups of coffee.

"Hope you still like yours black," Alex muttered as he thrust a cup into Titus' hands.

"I do. Thanks." Titus ushered his brother inside and closed the door. "I wasn't expecting this visit."

"I was out and about doing some things, and I prefer speaking face-to-face. But I don't have much time."

"Come into the living room and sit down a minute."

"Perfect."

Once they were seated, Titus turned to him. "What's going on?"

"I need you to keep an eye on Presley today. I have some things I need to do, but some threats have been made against us, and I don't feel right leaving Presley without any type of protection."

"Threats?" Was this a cover for something? Or were there actual threats he needed to know about? Either way—he didn't like the sound of this conversation.

Alex's lip twitched down in a quick frown. "Members of my organization often get threats because we're threatening the status quo. Most likely, nothing will come of it. But I have to be on the safe side—especially when it comes to Presley."

Titus' stomach turned at his words. "Of course. I'd be more than happy to keep an eye on Presley."

He couldn't help but wonder what Alex might be up to. He would tell the other guys on his Blackout team about it, and maybe someone could tail Alex. His brother was so manipulative that it was anyone's guess what was really going on.

"There's one other thing I thought I would let you know." Alex's gaze met Titus'. "Presley and I are going to get married tomorrow."

Titus' eyebrows shot up as he tried to feign surprise. "What? That's sudden."

"I know. But I don't know why I've put marriage off this long. I'm ready. I'm so glad you're okay with things between the two of us. It means the world to me to have your support."

"Of course." Titus forced the words out as he gripped his coffee cup.

"In other circumstances, I might ask you to be my best man. But, unfortunately, you'll be working during the ceremony." Alex took a sip of his drink.

That was because Alex was going to get married across town while this domestic terrorist event took place, wasn't he? It would give him the perfect alibi.

Anger burned through Titus' blood, but he couldn't say anything about it.

"I understand," he said instead.

"I was also wondering if you might take her by a bridal boutique. She needs to pick out a wedding dress for our wedding, and I've already made the appointment. I'd say one of her friends could go with her, but she's a bit of a loner."

Funny . . . Presley hadn't been a loner when Titus had known her. He had no doubt Alex had pushed her friends away. Had isolated her because it was easier to control someone when they were isolated.

Titus tried not to reveal any of those thoughts though as he nodded. "Of course. Whatever you need."

Although helping her pick out a dress for her wedding to Alex was the last thing he wanted to do, in the back of his mind Titus knew he wasn't going to let the wedding take place. So, he played along.

Alex took another sip of his coffee before standing and extending his hand. "Thank you. If you could pick her up at eight for church, that would be perfect."

"I would be more than happy to."

As Titus walked him to the door, Alex paused and sniffed.

"I like your cologne," he said. "It's a piney scent, isn't it?"

"It is. It's just something I picked up while I was stationed overseas."

"I like it."

What a strange statement, Titus thought as he watched his brother leave.

THIRTY-SEVEN

ALEX CALLED Presley first thing Sunday morning. She'd held her breath as she answered, certain he would tell her he knew about her escapades last night.

Instead, he'd said something popped up today, and he wouldn't be able to join her at church. He'd assigned Titus to escort her instead. And to take her dress shopping.

Her instincts had instantly gone on alert.

That didn't sound like something Alex would do.

She couldn't imagine why he'd ask Titus to keep an eye on her.

The whole thing had Presley on edge, even though she *was* looking forward to seeing Titus.

She hurried through her morning routine and got ready, trying to remain calm and not panic.

Right on time, Titus knocked on her door.

Presley rushed to open it, and her breath caught when she saw him on the other side.

He looked handsome in his black pants and button-up shirt. Then again, he always cleaned up nicely.

He leaned against the door frame, his eyebrows raised and a cautious look in his gaze. "I'm assuming you got the memo."

She nodded and pushed a stray hair behind her ear, her hand trembling as she did so. "I did. But I'm afraid something is up, Titus."

He stepped inside and shut the door. "That's what I think too. This whole request reeks of something fishy."

"I guess until then, we make the best of it?" She shrugged before grabbing her purse from the table near the door.

"I guess so. Looking on the bright side, at least I get to spend time with you."

Presley smiled, despite the situation.

Spending time with Titus *was* the one positive in this situation. "I agree."

Why couldn't this be her life? Why had she fallen for Alex when he offered her comfort after her mom died?

That one decision affected every aspect of her life today.

Ultimately, it had left her feeling trapped with no way out.

And Presley had no one to blame for it but herself.

It would be easy to blame Alex. He'd been charming and manipulative. But the choice to fall into his arms had been hers. She wished she'd been stronger.

She liked to think she was now.

But these next few days might test that theory.

She shoved those thoughts aside and glanced up at Titus. "Are you ready to go?"

His eyes were warm with affection as he nodded. "I am."

An image of her reaching up and planting a quick kiss on his lips filled her mind. She quickly shook away the thought.

Titus was right. They absolutely could *not* be affectionate with each other or entertain the idea of a relationship until Alex was out of her life.

She had to hold herself to a higher standard.

Before Titus opened the door, his phone rang. He held up a finger, silently asking her to wait a moment.

As soon as he began speaking into the phone, his voice turned grim.

Alarm spread through her as she anticipated the worst.

After he ended the call, he turned back to her. "That was my team leader. He heard from a police friend that they found another dead body that's most likely connected with The System."

"What?" she gasped.

Titus nodded, the look in his eyes serious. "The body . . . it belonged to Lars. He was shot point-blank approximately six hours ago."

There was too much to be worried about for Titus to relish his time with Presley.

Going to church with her had been nice, as had having lunch with her at a Mexican restaurant afterward.

But considering the circumstances . . . he hadn't been able to fully enjoy her company.

With any luck, their situation *would* be different soon.

Whatever The System was planning—The Great Awakening—the scheme was being set in place tomorrow.

Titus felt certain that after that, things would change.

He only hoped that they changed in the way he wanted them to.

He couldn't get Lars out of his mind. What had the man done to "warrant" his death? Had he betrayed The System? Not followed directions?

Titus' stomach knotted at the thought.

In the meantime, he kept his eyes open for anyone watching them.

Because he felt certain Alex had one of his guys keeping an eye on them.

As he and Presley finished eating every last tortilla chip—a tradition going back to when they'd dated—and he paid the bill, Presley looked at him, her expression growing serious.

"Alex told me that you're supposed to take me dress shopping so I can try on a few things," she started with a frown. "I know how terribly awkward that's going to be . . ."

Titus shrugged. He'd been thinking about it ever since Alex had told him, and he was working hard to keep his emotions out of this. But seeing Presley in a wedding dress? So she could marry someone other than him?

It wouldn't be easy.

Titus felt certain Alex was banking on that fact.

As he glanced at Presley, he put those thoughts aside. She didn't want to do this any more than he did, did she?

"I'll be okay," he insisted, lowering his voice. "I'll just keep telling myself that you're not going to marry Alex. I'll figure out a way to make sure you don't."

Presley stared at him another moment before nodding. "Okay."

Thirty minutes later, they arrived at a specialty wedding dress boutique on the outskirts of town. Their personal attendant, a woman named Lydia, had pulled out a few wedding gowns she thought Presley might like.

As Presley tried them on, Titus sat in a plush chair in a mirrored room, keeping guard for any trouble that might wander their way.

"Any luck so far?" Lydia asked Presley from the other side of a curtained area.

"I've tried on two, and I don't like them."

"Well, you could always show us so you could get our opinion." She glanced at Titus and smiled. "Although, it's not traditional for the groom to see the bride like this."

"Oh, I'm not the groom," Titus said—even though he wished he were. If life hadn't happened as it did . . . maybe he *would* be the soon-to-be groom.

But regret only burdened him right now—and he couldn't afford the distraction.

Lydia blushed. "I'm so sorry. The two of you have such great chemistry, I just assumed—"

"It's okay." He raised his hand to stop the woman before she could say anything else. "I'm the future brother-in-law, but we get that a lot."

She nodded apologetically before stepping away.

A moment later, Presley stepped from beyond the curtain, looking uncertain as she glanced around.

Titus' breath caught when he saw the strapless white gown that billowed at her hips. Simple lines that accentuated all her best features.

She looked gorgeous.

More than gorgeous.

Seeing her in that dress was everything Titus had dreamed about since the day they'd first met.

"Do you hate it?" Presley almost looked self-conscious as she glanced down at the gown.

Titus shook his head, trying to control himself—to hide his attraction before Lydia assumed anything else. "No. Hating it is the last thing I feel. You look . . . amazing."

Her cheeks flushed. "Thank you." Presley stared at him another moment before swallowing, her throat appearing tight. "I should go change. But I don't want to waste this dress on Alex. I don't want to wear it for him at all."

His pulse kicked up a notch.

If Titus had anything to do with it, she wouldn't.

Before he could say anything else, his phone rang.

He saw it was Brandon and quickly answered. "What's going on?"

"I thought I'd let you know that we talked to Senator Gately and told him about the situation."

"Did he cancel his rally?" Titus waited, hoping this attack could be thwarted before it even began.

"No, Gately said that he can't let bullies make him back down."

Titus tried not to flinch at his words. "Even if his life is on the line? Or the lives of innocent people who might come out to support him?"

"He said he's going to up his security measures, but he's not backing down to bullies. Not now and not ever."

Titus didn't know whether to appreciate that about the man or to reprimand him.

But without that rally being canceled . . . they were going to have to think of another way to stop this terrorist attack before it happened.

BEFORE GOING BACK into the dressing room, Presley paused. Titus got off the phone and glanced at Lydia. Clearly, he couldn't share whatever he'd just heard.

But concern filled his gaze.

Before she could ask any questions, Lydia stepped forward and placed a veil on her head. Then she stepped back, hands clasped in front of her, and practically beamed as she stared at Presley.

"Now it's just perfect," Lydia murmured.

Presley glanced in the mirror and sucked in a breath.

It was perfect.

She looked just like the bride she'd always dreamed about being.

A surge of bittersweetness rose in her.

How could everything be so perfect and so wrong at the same time?

Titus rose and stood behind her, staring at her reflection also. As he did, their gazes met in the mirror.

As she stared at him, she forgot everything else.

Something real—something strong—passed between them.

They both knew the truth.

Planning her wedding was something the two of them should share.

Not something that she and Alex should be experiencing.

A rush of loss filled Presley until she felt as if she were drowning in a sea of regrets.

Titus opened his mouth to speak, but the words seemed to catch in his throat. "Presley . . ."

Her breath caught as she waited for him to continue.

Would he confirm her thoughts?

Admit that he shared her feelings?

Or was she alone in this moment? Was Titus lost in his job—just as Alex had goaded her with before he'd made his move? Could Titus work in security and still make her a priority?

So many thoughts swam through her mind. She

could hardly make her way through the muck to get to the surface for air.

"You look out of this world," a deep voice said.

Presley flinched as the words hurled through the room.

She turned and spotted Alex standing in the doorway, looking Presley up and down with admiration.

The breath whooshed from her lungs as Presley realized Alex may have seen too much when he walked in. What if he'd noticed the way she looked at Titus? The way Titus looked at her?

She had to pull herself together.

Titus took a step back, allowing her to turn.

Putting on the familiar façade, Presley stepped close enough for Alex to give her a kiss—one that lingered entirely too long for her comfort.

"I wasn't expecting to see you here," she murmured as she stared up at him.

"I got finished with my meeting early, so I decided to come join in the fun. I'm so glad that I did." He looked at her with admiration again before glancing at Titus.

Her lungs tightened when she saw something change in his gaze.

Had Alex seen the look between her and Titus? Did he know somehow that she and Titus still had feelings for each other?

She tried her best to hide her affection for Titus. But Alex seemed to have a sixth sense about him sometimes.

"I didn't think you were supposed to see the bride in the wedding dress before the wedding day." Titus' voice sounded stiff, as if he felt the same way she did.

"I think that's just on the wedding day, right? Anyway, I'm paying for the dress so I figured I could see it." Alex twirled Presley around as he admired her. "It's everything I ever dreamed about. Do you like it?"

Her throat tightened even more. She *did* like this dress. In fact, she loved it.

But she didn't want to wear it for Alex.

Maybe she should grab one she didn't like. Maybe she should wear that instead. Fake it. Pretend another gown was her favorite.

"I do have a couple of other options." She nodded back to the curtained-off dressing room.

"No." Alex shook his head, not a hint of doubt in his gaze. "Only this one will do. You look like a million bucks. Will you wear this one for me? Please?"

Even though he said the words as if she had a choice, Presley knew she didn't.

Trying on these dresses brought her back to her

pageant days. Days when her mom had dressed her up as if she were a baby doll. Back to when her hair had been pinned, she'd been spray tanned, and then she'd been paraded around to be judged on her looks.

She never wanted that kind of life again . . . yet here she was. All grown up. Different circumstances.

But the same position.

She forced herself to nod. "If this makes you happy, then this is the dress I'll wear."

A wide grin spread across Alex's face, and he turned toward the attendant. "We'll take it. It fits like a glove, which is perfect—especially since we're not going to have any time for alterations."

Presley swallowed hard, trying not to show her apprehension. "If that's what you want."

"I do. More than anything." Alex turned to Titus. "I can take over from here. But thank you for your help today. It means a lot to me."

Titus' broad shoulders were notably tense as he strode toward them. "I hope everything worked out at your emergency meeting."

Was Titus still thinking about Lars?

Had Alex killed the other security guard? Or had he sent one of his people to do so?

Titus gave Presley one more look before stepping back. "You two have fun."

"I'll need you tomorrow morning," Alex called. "I'll text you the details."

Titus nodded again as he headed toward the door.

Presley instantly missed him and wished things were different—she wished it so hard that her soul seemed to ache at the thought.

She had to figure out a way to make sure that things were ultimately different.

The last thing that Titus wanted was to leave.

He wanted to stay with Presley. To pretend like no one else existed. That no other problems lingered on the horizon. And that Alex wasn't a part of their lives.

But those things were foolish hopes.

Especially considering the stakes.

He strode from the bridal boutique back to his truck. As he glanced across the parking lot, he spotted Thomas in his coupe.

Good. Titus felt better knowing that someone besides Alex was keeping an eye on Presley.

Titus would stay and watch her himself, but Alex had clearly dismissed him.

For now, Titus needed to head back to his apartment to change before meeting with his team to figure out their next plan of action.

He gripped the steering wheel as he headed down the road.

His brother was a vile man. He didn't deserve someone like Presley. But his brother was the type who got away with everything. He seemed untouchable.

Whatever Alex and his friends were planning, Titus felt certain his brother would walk away unscathed.

Even as a child, Alex had been like that. He'd broken their father's favorite desk lamp and had managed to blame it on Titus. When Alex was a little older, he had deliberately set off the house alarm and said it was Titus' fault. Alex had said that the scratch on their dad's Mercedes got there because Titus had accidentally run his bike handle across the door.

He frowned at the memories, at the manipulation, as he parked in the lot adjacent to his complex. But as he strode toward his apartment, his shoulders felt heavy and burdened with the weight of everything that was happening.

As he opened the door to his apartment, he froze.

Something didn't feel right.

He glanced around, not bothering to flick the lights on.

What was it that was making his nerves stand on edge?

Before he could figure it out, shadows shifted around him.

Surrounded him.

He prepared himself for another attack.

Instead, he heard, "FBI! Put your hands in the air. Titus Armstrong, you're being taken in under multiple federal terrorism charges."

TITUS FELT sweat bead across his forehead as the FBI surrounded him. "What kind of terrorism charges am I facing?"

The same FBI agent who'd shown up at the compound—Murdoch—stared at him. "We found bomb-making materials in your closet."

"Bomb-making materials?" Then all at once it hit him.

He'd been set up.

The only reason Alex had asked Titus to spend time with Presley today was so Titus would be out of his apartment and Alex's guys could come in to plant evidence that made him look guilty.

Was that what Alex had grabbed from the cabin while Presley hid under the bed?

Probably.

Titus felt like a fool.

He should have expected this from Alex. This was just like something his brother would do.

Special Agent Murdoch handcuffed him and read him his rights before leading him from the apartment.

Several neighbors stuck their heads out their doors to see what was going on.

Titus kept his chin up high, determined not to show any signs of guilt.

"What kind of evidence could you possibly have against me to get a warrant to come in here?" Titus asked.

"We looked into your background," Murdoch said. "Saw you had a tough time in the military. We checked your credit card records and saw that you've been purchasing caustic substances. Checked your computer history and saw you'd been researching water reservoirs."

"I'm being set up," Titus said through clenched teeth. "I didn't buy any of those things. I didn't leave those materials there. Alex Armstrong—my brother —did."

"We'll have plenty of time to talk things through once we take you down to the field office."

Titus' mind continued to race.

This was bad.

Really bad.

Alex was a smart man. He'd known exactly how to get Titus out of the way.

Had this been his plan all along?

Probably.

And if this had been Alex's plan for Titus, what exactly was his brother planning for Presley?

Titus didn't know.

But suddenly, his world felt like it had been turned upside down.

The wedding dress rested like a corpse in the backseat of Alex's car.

Seeing it solidified what would be taking place tomorrow.

No, she told herself. This wasn't the end of her story.

She could still say no—right up until that very moment of the ceremony.

But, for now, she needed to keep playing along.

"I thought we could go back to my place and unwind a little," Alex said as they started down the road. He acted as if nothing had happened and like all was well.

Certainly, he knew better.

She frowned at the thought of spending more time with him.

Between church, lunch, and dress shopping, most of the day was gone. The sun was already sinking in the sky.

"It's been a long time since the two of us have had any quality time together," Alex continued. "Besides, we have wedding plans to talk about."

Wedding plans were the last thing she wanted to talk about. But Presley only smiled.

Thirty minutes later, they arrived at Alex's place, a modern, two-story house in an affluent neighborhood.

She settled on the couch with a glass of water and took a long sip as she tried to compose herself.

Before she and Alex could talk, his phone rang, and he excused himself to answer. But when Alex returned to the room, his expression was solemn—almost mournful.

He sat beside her, propping his elbows on his legs as he leaned closer.

"I'm not sure how to tell you this." Alex rubbed a hand over his mouth as if uncomfortable. "I'm not sure I believe it myself."

Her anxiety thrummed harder. "What's going on?"

"I just got a call from an associate about Titus. The FBI arrested him."

Her throat thickened until she could hardly breathe. "What?"

"Apparently, the feds got a tip, which led them to some suspicious supplies in Titus' closet. They found plans to bomb the capitol building in North Carolina and sabotage a water reservoir."

Presley grasped her throat, which felt like it was thickening with every second. "He would never do that."

"I know, I know." Alex raised his hand and patted the air as if to calm her down. "I have trouble believing it also. But you and I both know that the military changed him. He's not the same person he used to be."

"Alex . . . even if Titus wasn't the same person, he would never do this. You know that."

"The battlefield can change people, my love. I admire the fact you believe in him so much. But it looks like the feds have an airtight case against him."

Indignation rose in her. "You're just going to let them charge him with this?"

"No, I'm going to go down there and offer to represent him."

More alarm flooded through Presley. *That* was also a terrible idea.

But she knew she couldn't talk Alex out of it. His mind was made up.

Instead, she stood. "Let me go with you."

He swung his head back and forth, a firm look in his gaze. "There's no reason for you to go. You'll just be standing around doing nothing . . ."

Presley had to think of a way to get to Titus without showing her hand. "Please, Alex . . . I know he's your brother. If Titus ruins his reputation, he could tarnish yours as well. Let me be there for you."

A sickly feeling swirled in her gut as her statement hung in the air.

This could backfire.

It could majorly backfire.

She was waiting for Alex to put her in the hospital. She could perfectly envision him rehearsing excuses with her as to what had happened.

I fell down the stairs and broke my arm. I dropped the pan I was cooking with and burned myself. I tripped and busted my lip.

Presley stared at Alex and waited for his answer, praying he didn't see through her.

And praying she didn't pay the price for her request.

Not yet.

Hopefully, not ever.

TITUS HAD BEEN SITTING in the interrogation room for two hours already. FBI agents had asked him the same questions over and over. And he'd answered those questions in the same way over and over again also.

Titus had called Brandon, who told him to tell the FBI the truth.

So, Titus had. He'd explained his role with Blackout. Explained his relationship with Alex. Explained everything that he was investigating and all the evidence and theories.

But the agents remained skeptical.

As they left the room, Titus leaned forward on the table. He couldn't move from it. He'd been handcuffed to a bar there.

His head pounded. Would he really be framed for this planned domestic terrorist attack?

Titus had known his brother was a snake, but he'd never thought Alex would take things this far.

Meanwhile, while the FBI was distracted by Titus, The System was going to enact their real plan.

And they just might get away with it.

Oh, God . . . crying out to Him seemed the only thing Titus could do right now.

That and get an attorney.

Brandon was already working on sending someone over.

But to his surprise, an hour later the feds announced that Alex had shown up.

Titus had to think quickly. Did he continue on this route with his brother? Or did he unleash every harsh thing he'd bottled up inside him and give his brother a real piece of his mind?

As Presley's image came to his mind, Titus knew what he had to do.

He had to keep up this charade.

For her sake.

There would be a time for retribution later.

But for now, Titus would play dumb. Pretend with his brother that he didn't know what was going on.

FBI agents shouldn't be able to hear their conversation, and Titus was sure Alex would tell him to not say anything else.

Titus only hoped this worked.

As Alex stepped in the room, Titus looked up, not bothering to hide the exhaustion in his gaze.

"I heard." Alex set his briefcase on the interrogation table. "You haven't told them anything, have you?"

"How did you even hear?" Titus' mind raced. He hadn't called his brother.

Did his brother have an inside connection?

Just how deep did The System run?

The thought caused his throat to go dry.

Was that why the FBI hadn't been able to get a warrant to get into the compound yesterday? Did The System know someone within the legal system?

"I have some connections." Alex shrugged off the question. "But it doesn't matter. Don't say anything else to the feds. They'll only trap you and twist your words around to make you seem guilty."

"I know." If that was true, then Alex should be a fed because he was a master at doing those things also.

Alex lowered himself into the chair across from Titus, and the two locked gazes. "These charges are serious."

Titus nodded again, his chest tightening at the reminder. "I know."

"You'll be facing life in prison." Alex sighed and leaned back as if gathering his thoughts. "How did those things even get into your apartment?"

Anger flashed inside Titus, but he tried not to show it. He rubbed his jaw instead. "I have no idea."

Alex frowned and tapped his finger against the table. "It sounds like someone has a vendetta against you. Who has access to your apartment?"

"No one. No one has access to my place. And no one I know has a vendetta against me."

Except you, Titus added silently.

"Certainly, you made enemies as a SEAL."

Titus shrugged. "I did. But none who would do this."

"How can you be so sure?"

Titus needed to back off. Alex's theory made sense. If Titus protested too much, it would only seem suspicious. "I guess I can't."

"That seems like a real possibility to me. After all, you put terrorists behind bars—if not worse, correct?"

"Correct."

His brother leaned in. "We're going to get to the bottom of this. I promise you that."

Titus wasn't so sure.

If Alex had his way, Titus would end up in prison for the rest of his life.

He had no doubt his brother would delight in that happening—in finally putting his little brother in his place while permanently keeping him away from Presley.

Presley paced the front lobby of the FBI office.

Alex had agreed she could come as long as she stayed out of the way.

But anxiety had bubbled inside her until she nearly felt beside herself.

How could Alex have done this to Titus?

Her hatred of the man grew even more.

Yes, hatred.

Presley knew the Bible told her not to hate anyone, but it would take time to get over this and forgive Alex—*if* she could ever do that at all.

Alex didn't deserve her forgiveness.

But she'd have to work that out later.

Right now, she needed to concentrate on Titus.

He wasn't going to get out of here anytime soon, was he?

In fact, the FBI could still be holding him

tomorrow morning when she was supposed to marry Alex.

More nausea swirled in her stomach.

She couldn't wait for Titus to figure out how to stop this.

Presley had to do something on her own.

But what? What could she do?

Taking any action at this point could very well get her killed.

But the risk seemed worth it.

Especially if innocent lives were saved.

Presley's mind raced as she contemplated what to do.

Only one idea came to mind.

Her stomach roiled at the thought.

Her plan would be dangerous.

But it was the only thing that made sense.

CHAPTER
FORTY-ONE

TITUS WAS ready for his brother to leave, but Alex stayed with him at the FBI field office for two more hours. Agents continued to try to question him, but Titus refused to answer—just as he'd been instructed.

He obviously wasn't getting anywhere telling the truth.

He wanted to talk to Brandon again. To see if his teammate had figured anything out yet. To see if he'd talked to his contact within the FBI.

But he couldn't bring that up in front of Alex.

"They can hold you for forty-eight hours," Alex said. "Presley is very concerned."

Titus stared at his brother, searching his gaze. Did his brother know something was going on? That Titus cared for Presley? That Presley still cared for him?

He couldn't be sure, but it was a definite possibility.

Titus cleared his burning throat. "Is she here?"

"She's waiting in the lobby. I told her not to come, but she insisted. Said she wanted to be here to support me during this hard time. My reputation could very well take a hit after news of this goes public, you know."

Titus' heart beat harder. His brother was a malevolent narcissist who thought only about himself.

If Presley had indeed said those words, it was only because she knew how to speak to Alex's ego.

Another moment of apprehension flashed through Titus.

What would Alex do to Presley if he found out the truth? If he found out the two of them had feelings for each other?

Dread pooled in his stomach.

It wouldn't be good.

And Titus would be helpless to do anything about it.

As the taxi driver pulled to a stop, Presley opened the door and handed him some money. "Keep the change."

As he pulled away, she straightened her skirt and looked at the house in the distance.

She was out of her league coming here.

But she had to do *something*, and this seemed like the best option.

No doubt, Titus had told the FBI already what was really going on. It seemed apparent that the feds didn't believe him.

But maybe, if she could get through to someone else in power, this whole plan could be stopped.

She stared at Senator Gately's house. The all-brick structure looked regal, standing at three stories, with elegant landscape lighting and artistic flowerbeds.

Presley had found the senator's address through a database on the law firm's network. Alex was one of the senator's donors.

Lifting up a prayer and dragging in every last ounce of courage, she started to the door. She didn't know for sure that the senator was home tonight, nor did she know how well he'd receive what she told him.

But talking to him was worth a shot.

At this point, Presley had nothing to lose.

She strode across the driveway to the front door and knocked.

A moment later, Keri, the senator's wife, answered. The woman was tall and slender with short, dark-brown hair and a quiet demeanor. Presley had met her once before at a political fundraiser she'd attended with Alex.

"I'm sorry to bother you, but I was hoping to talk to your husband," Presley started.

"Who are you?" Keri stared at her, clearly cautious.

The senator appeared behind his wife, wrapping a protective arm around her waist. "Can I help you?"

"I'm sorry. I'm Alex Armstrong's fiancée. Presley Lennox."

The man's eyes widened. "That's right. Any friend of Alex is a friend of mine. Please, come in."

Presley rubbed her hands together, feeling the perspiration on her palms.

Her knees practically wobbled as she thought about the impact of what she was about to do. It was too late to go back now.

Keri led them into the living room, and Presley lowered herself onto the couch there. Then Keri excused herself, leaving only Senator Gately and Presley to speak.

"What brings you out here?" the senator started, his gaze curious. "I don't see your car, and I don't see Alex."

"I actually took a taxi. There's an urgent matter I need to speak with you about."

"Of course. What's on your mind?"

She licked her lips, which felt unusually dry. "I don't know how to say this, so I'm just going to get to the point. I believe that there's going to be an assassination attempt on you at your rally tomorrow —most likely a bomb."

He nodded, appearing surprisingly unalarmed. "I actually heard something about that, and I've upped my security for the event."

"That's good but . . ." She licked her lips again. "I know this may sound hard to believe, but I believe Alex and some of his friends are planning it."

The senator chuckled and shook his head. "You're right. I do find that hard to believe. Alex has always been one of my biggest supporters."

"Maybe on paper he has been. But he's developed some radical ideas in recent years. He'd like to see the political system in our country change. I believe he's willing to go through drastic measures in order to make this happen."

"Like an assassination attempt?" The senator narrowed his eyes as if uncertain.

Presley nodded, knowing how far out her words sounded. Anyone in the senator's shoes would be skeptical. "Yes. I'm afraid so."

"What makes you think that?" He continued to

study her as if trying to figure out if she'd lost her marbles or not.

"Alex and his friends have been meeting in private. Collecting supplies and floorplans and contacts. Based on everything I've heard, this ordeal —called The Great Awakening—is set to happen tomorrow. It's going to be serious."

He narrowed his eyes with thought. "If you don't mind me asking, why are you telling me this instead of the FBI?"

"I've tried to get other people to listen, but they won't. So, I thought I'd come straight to you. I hoped if I did, you might be able to help. I don't want to see any harm come to you or any of your supporters."

Senator Gately blinked several times before slowly nodding. "I appreciate that. I'm sorry if I don't seem to be acting more urgently. It's going to take a moment for this to sink in."

"I understand that it's a lot, and I'm sorry to throw it all on you at once. I just didn't know what else to do."

"I have a contact I can consult about this." Senator Gately rose, his face lined with tension. "I need to make a call, but I'll be right back. In the meantime, try to calm down. You did the right thing by coming to me."

But Presley's mind continued to race.

Had she done the right thing?

She prayed she had.

But until everybody was safe, she would be on edge.

FORTY-TWO

FINALLY, at three a.m., Titus was released from FBI custody. It was only after Colton Locke, the Blackout CEO, had called his FBI contact and explained the situation.

Brandon had been waiting for Titus outside a back exit and shared the news with him.

They'd also decided to keep his release under wraps—just in case Alex had someone working on the inside.

"Thanks for coming," Titus muttered as the two fell into step beside each other and headed to the parking lot. "I'm glad they released me, but I'm afraid I'm still going to be framed for this."

Brandon's shoulders stiffened. "We're going to do everything we can to ensure that doesn't happen. We got you into this mess. We'll get you out."

Titus paused beside Brandon's SUV. "I know you said Colton called in a favor . . . does that mean the FBI is actually going to listen to what I told them?"

"That's what we're hoping," Brandon said as they climbed into the SUV and slammed the doors. "Look, we don't have a lot of answers right now. I could take you back to your place, but I'm sure that's now considered a crime scene. How about if I take you back to our place instead?"

His throat tightened at the mundane thought of returning to the apartment. Too much was on the line. "I need to see Presley."

Brandon let out a long breath. "I know Thomas was trying to keep an eye on her, but with all the craziness, he lost her again."

"What?" Alarm raced through him.

"He said he was sitting outside this whole time. But he never saw her leave with Alex."

"I need to make sure she's okay. I have a feeling Alex knows what's happening here."

"Whatever you need me to do," Brandon said.

"I'll try her cell first." Titus dialed her number, but there was no answer.

Instead, he pulled up the security camera feed from the device he'd set up in her hallway. He scanned the last couple of hours—but there was no Presley. She wasn't there.

Titus' heart pumped harder as he fought a spirit of defeat.

Then he realized where she might be.

"Alex's," Titus muttered, running a hand through his hair. "I need to see if she's there."

Brandon stared at him a moment. "Are you sure that's a good idea? If Alex sees you there, you're going to have a lot of explaining to do."

Titus didn't care right now. The only thing he cared about was Presley. "I know. I'll think of something. But I have to know she's okay."

Brandon started the engine. "I'll take you there then. You'll need backup."

Titus gave Brandon directions, and a few minutes later they pulled to a stop a block away from Alex's house. It looked the same as it had a few years ago when Titus had last visited.

His house looked dark, and his car wasn't out front.

"Where would Alex be at this time of night?" Brandon muttered.

"Good question."

Brandon handed Titus an extra gun. "Just in case."

Climbing from the SUV, they crept toward the house, careful to remain in the shadows.

A number pad stared at them from the front door.

Titus should be able to figure this out. He knew all of Alex's codes from when they were kids. He'd probably have three chances before being locked out or having an alarm of some sort go off.

"You think you can do this?" Brandon asked quietly.

Titus nodded. "I do."

Taking a deep breath, he typed in Alex's birthday.

The lock slid open.

He released the air from his lungs.

It was one more obstacle out of the way.

But the hardest was yet to come.

He and Brandon slipped inside the quiet house.

Motioning to each other, they split up to search the place.

Given the fact Alex's car wasn't here, Titus felt certain his brother wasn't home.

But they had to be sure.

They searched the downstairs and then the upstairs.

The place was empty.

Just as Brandon and Titus met back downstairs, a shadow appeared in the doorway.

A shadow with a gun.

Presley looked up as Senator Gately strode back into the room. "I made a few phone calls, and I think we've got this under control now. You don't have anything else to worry about."

Her shoulders softened, even though his words sounded too good to be true. Could it really be that easy?

"You called the FBI? They believed you?" She needed to make sure she'd understood correctly.

"Not exactly." He shrugged. "I called someone even better."

Presley blinked, trying to figure out where he was going with this.

As he nodded behind him, someone stepped out from his office.

Presley rose to her feet as the air left her lungs. "Alex . . ."

Her mind raced.

What was he doing here?

None of this made sense . . .

"You really thought you were going to be able to sell me out like that?" Alex's voice sounded deep, gravelly—almost a growl.

As Alex stepped closer, her throat tightened. Her muscles snapped tight. Her heart raced out of control.

Presley glanced back at Senator Gately, expecting to see fear on his face.

Instead, a grin curled his lips.

She gaped.

"You're in on this . . ." The words came out fast.

She couldn't believe what she was seeing with her own eyes. How could this be happening?

"There's nothing to build sympathy like an attempt on your life. In fact, it may be my key to being reelected." He smirked with satisfaction.

Her gaze darted back and forth between the two men. "You guys are in on this together. You share the same ideological beliefs." She rubbed the skin between her eyes, feeling an ache beginning to pound at her temples. "I can't believe I didn't see it."

Alex ran his fingers down her jaw. "You were just supposed to sit back and be pretty."

She didn't try to hide her flinch this time. "There's more to me than just a pretty face."

He ran his hand lower, his fingers splaying across the back of her neck and his thumb sliding below her chin.

Her breath caught as she waited.

Apprehension suffocated her.

As Alex glared, his thumb pressed against her windpipe, threatening to cut her air off. "You're only supposed to be who I say you are. I don't know what's gotten into you lately. Maybe it's the fact that Titus came back into your life."

Immediately, concern for Titus became her only focus. "We're just friends. You know that. We haven't crossed any lines."

"But you want to, and I can't let that happen." Alex pressed on her windpipe harder, totally cutting off her air supply.

She gasped, her lungs desperate for oxygen. Her arms flailed as she tried to shove Alex away.

But she was no match for him.

"Alex!" Senator Gately called. "There will be time for that later. Right now, we have other matters to attend to. We have other loose ends that we need to clear up."

As Presley clawed at Alex, stars formed in her eyes.

Everything around her spun.

Then Alex released her, practically shoving her away from him as if she were poison.

She fell limp on the couch as she drank in deep gulps of air.

"You're right." Alex glared at her, vengeance in his gaze. "I'll have time to deal with her later. For now, we need to think of something to do with her."

Senator Gately nodded, a new gleam in his eyes as he said, "I think I have the perfect idea."

"I WOULDN'T PULL that gun if I were you," a deep voice said.

But it didn't belong to Alex.

Had the FBI followed Titus and Brandon here? Were they just waiting for Titus to mess up so they could bring him in again?

Titus wasn't sure, but he raised his hands in the air as he braced himself for whatever would come next.

The man in the doorway reached for the light switch, and the bulb overhead flashed on.

Titus blinked a few times before muttering, "Jesse?"

Alex must have sent one of his lackeys here to keep an eye on things. Now Jesse would do Alex's dirty work and finish Titus off.

"If you promise not to make any moves, you can put your arms down." Jesse stepped closer, gun still in hand.

Titus wasn't sure where Jesse was going with this. He and Brandon glanced at each other before nodding and lowering their arms back to their sides.

"What are you doing here?" Jesse demanded as he paused in front of them.

"We're looking for Presley," Titus answered. "I believe she's in danger."

"So you broke in?" Jesse narrowed his gaze.

Titus knew he needed to be very careful as he answered. "I believe she's in imminent danger, and there's no time to waste in finding out."

Jesse stared at him again, still nodding and holding his gun.

"Look, I don't want any trouble," Titus said, realizing this was taking entirely too much time. "I just don't want anyone else to get hurt."

"Then you and I want the same thing." Jesse raised his chin, his gaze coolly assessing.

Titus' spine stiffened. Had he heard the man correctly? What did that even mean?

Jesse reached into his pocket and pulled something out. A moment later, he flashed his badge. "I'm actually Special Agent Jesse Marx with the FBI. I've been working undercover for the past three months to try to bring these guys down."

"What?" Titus could hardly believe his ears.

But it looked like they had a lot to talk about.

Alex gripped Presley's arm so hard that she had to resist a squeal. In a whirlwind, he began dragging her toward the back of the house. "The senator told me about the perfect place I could keep you until this blows over."

"Until what blows over?" Her thoughts raced.

"Until we can get married in the morning."

She dug her heels into the floor. "We're not going to get married. You can't possibly think that I will after all of this."

He stopped and turned to her, anger flashing in his gaze. "You don't have any other choice."

She twisted her head, wondering where he was going with this. "What do you mean by that?"

"I mean, I have an inside man at the FBI. If you don't do what I ask, there will be consequences."

Her breath caught. "You mean you're going to hurt Titus?"

"I'm smart. You don't think I see the way the two

of you look at each other? You don't think I smelled his cologne in your apartment after he had been there? I'm not a fool. And I don't appreciate being treated like one."

"If you've seen all that, why do you still want to marry me?"

"Because you're mine." His voice hardened. "Nothing will ever change that. Ever. Do you understand?"

He shook her as he asked the question.

She felt rattled to the core.

She had seen evil in his eyes before.

But never had they looked this empty and soulless.

Presley could hardly control the terror that raced through her.

Before she could even respond, Alex's grip on her arm tightened, and he continued pulling her through the house.

He opened a door and shoved her inside a small closet.

As darkness surrounded her, something clicked in place. She'd been locked in here, hadn't she?

And this was where she'd wait until it was time to get ready to get married.

Despair caught in her throat, the emotion nearly choking her. What was she going to do?

If she didn't marry Alex then Titus would die.

She couldn't let that happen.

But she was out of ideas as to what else to do right now.

FORTY-FOUR

"WAIT . . ." Titus stared at Jesse. "You've been working for the FBI this whole time?"

"That's right. I've been deep undercover trying to find out information about what these guys are doing. I wondered whose side you were on."

"You know that I don't support them, right?" Titus clarified just to make sure that they were on the same page.

"I do now."

"Why did you go to Presley's door that night?" His thoughts continued to race as he tried to figure out whether or not he could really trust this guy.

"I saw you go up to her apartment. I wasn't sure what was going on, and I knew Presley was an asset. I wanted to keep an eye on her. Then you showed up, and I figured out you were one of the good guys."

"When the FBI came to the gate at the compound . . . did they know who you were?"

"No, and I was afraid my operation was going to be blown. Thankfully, it wasn't." Jesse let out a sigh. "I heard everything that happened today. We've got to stop these guys."

Titus drew in a deep breath as the urgency of the situation hit him again. "Last I heard, Senator Gately won't cancel the rally."

"I know. My colleagues are going to have bomb-sniffing dogs on-site. We're going to do whatever we can to stop this attack."

"Presley said she overheard them saying something about speakers. Do you know if anyone else is lined up to give a speech besides Gately?"

Jesse nodded. "From what I've heard, other people are going to be speaking in support of him. I don't like any of this. But it's out of my hands to stop the rally from happening. In fact, I've been praying for rain because it seems like only something supernatural will ensure this doesn't happen."

Titus glanced at his watch. "It's already five a.m. The rally is supposed to happen at ten. Speaking of which, what are *you* doing here?"

"After you left the compound, they had us load a whole bunch of boxes into a van. A man I've never seen before drove off with them. I came here to see if I could find them. But I couldn't."

"Was Lars with you? Do you know what happened to him?"

"Only that he was killed."

Titus rubbed his neck as he realized how much time this conversation was wasting. "I'd love to chat more, but I need to find Presley. Alex is forcing her to marry him in the morning, and I have to stop it."

Jesse's eyebrows flickered upward. "It sounds like we have a lot of things that we need to stop."

"You can say that again," Titus muttered. "And we have no time to waste. I'd say we need to get busy."

Presley wasn't sure how long she had been in the closet. Sometimes it felt like mere moments. Other times it felt like hours.

She only knew the space was small. She couldn't even stretch out her legs when she sat on the floor.

She'd already searched the inside of the place, looking for anything she might be able to use as a weapon.

But the space was empty.

And the house was quiet, almost as if no one else were here.

Presley was nearly certain Senator Gately and his wife had already gone to get ready for the rally. She had no idea what Alex might be doing right now.

She only knew that she thought she was going to throw up.

Getting married under duress? Did that even count under the law? Was her saying, "I do" and an official signing off on it the only thing that mattered? And where was Alex even going to find an official?

Whichever way Presley looked at the situation, she couldn't see a way out.

She knew she had to fight. She had to do whatever she could to stop this from happening.

As the thoughts continued to race through her head, she heard footsteps. She rushed to her feet and braced herself for whatever might happen next.

The door flew open, and Alex stood there with something in his hands.

Her wedding dress.

Her heart sank with despair and anxiety threaded across her chest.

"It's almost time," he said. "I need you to get ready. Looking like you do right now won't work."

She only stared at him. Had he lost his mind?

Maybe. Or maybe his mind had never truly been there in the first place.

"Where are you even going to find someone who will marry us right now?"

A glimmer filled his eyes. "I have my sources. A judge, actually."

Her heart pounded in her ears. The System did have a judge on the inside, didn't they? They were using him to get what they wanted.

Just how many more people in positions of power were involved?

A judge. A senator. An FBI agent.

These were some of the unnamed core members.

The gravity of the situation hit her again.

As Alex grabbed her arm and pulled her from the closet, she tried to resist but it was no use. He was entirely too strong for her.

"Don't you want to be there for the rally today?" she asked instead.

"Why are you concerned?"

"I just thought it was important to you."

"No, it's important that I'm not there. I want to be as far away from that event as I can be."

"Because you and your friends are planning something terrible—something where innocent people are going to be hurt."

"It will never be traced back to us. In fact, this will

all look like it happened because of another terrorist group. Then my friends and I are going to ride in like knights on white horses and save the day. We'll be heroes, and people will turn to us to get answers. And that's when we can truly begin shifting the policies that we would like to see changed."

More nausea gurgled up inside her. "You've really thought all this through, haven't you?"

"We have some of the best minds in this country today. Of course, we've thought this through."

"But . . ."

He pushed her into a bedroom. "There are no buts about it. I need you to get changed. We only have two hours. So, chop chop, my love. Chop chop."

JESSE LOWERED HIS PHONE. "I just had one of my guys review some footage from outside the FBI building. It shows a taxi driver pulling up to get Presley."

Titus' pulse quickened. "Where did the taxi driver take her? Is there footage of that also?"

"There is. This is the weird part," Jesse said. "It looks like he took her to Senator Gately's house."

"What? Why would she go there?"

"Maybe she realized what was happening, and she went to try to warn him," Brandon suggested.

Titus nodded slowly. "You're probably right. That makes the most sense. But why would she still be there? The senator's rally is supposed to start in two hours."

"I'm sorry Titus, but we don't have that answer.

But all our teams are going to the rally," Brandon said. "Plus, the FBI is going to be on patrol. Hopefully, we'll be able to stop whatever plan these guys have set in motion."

"So, that means I can go after Presley?" He stared at Brandon.

Brandon nodded. "Yes. Go find Presley. Stop Alex from forcing her into marriage."

"Are you sure you don't need all your resources at the site?"

"Now that we know the FBI is actually listening, I think we'll be okay. Just save your girl."

Presley stared at herself in the mirror.

Here she was wearing the perfect gown. Looking like the perfect bride.

And all she wanted to do was cry. To tear the dress off and run.

But Alex stood beside her, holding a gun. Showing her pictures of Titus from the FBI office. Making it clear he had an inside guy who could finish his brother off if it came down to it.

"Are you ready?" Alex moved until he was behind her.

His body heat prickled her skin, and his lips grazed her neck until she wanted to throw up.

"You look beautiful," he murmured.

She stiffened. As one of his arms slipped around her waist, the other still held the weapon, the gun's barrel entirely too close to her heart.

"The judge is waiting," he continued. "I promise you we'll be happy, my love."

Presley knew she would *never* be happy. Not with Alex.

But it would do no good to tell him that.

"Did you kill all those people?" Her voice wavered as she asked the question.

He stiffened. "You really want to talk about that now?"

She turned toward him, desperate to know the truth—to see it in his gaze. "Yes, I do. Did you kill that reporter?"

Alex stepped back, his voice calm and casual still, as if they were talking about picking up groceries or something mundane. "Celeste wanted to leave us. I couldn't let that happen. Loyalty is valued in this organization, in case you didn't know. Celeste started off so strong. But we could tell she was beginning to crack."

"So, you killed her yourself?" Presley searched his gaze for the truth.

He scoffed. "No, of course not. I had my guys do that. Who do you think I am?"

"And John McNally? Did you kill him?"

His eyebrows shot up as if her words had caught him off guard. "I'm surprised you even know who he is."

"I know a lot of stuff."

He quickly recovered, all emotion disappearing. "He was going to sell us out. That was a grave mistake on his part."

"And Lars?"

"Lars knew too much. His hands were too dirty, and he was a liability. We couldn't take any chances." His gaze darkened. "Now, enough talking. This is such an exciting day with so much going on. One thing for sure, we will never forget this date. Nor will a lot of people."

Presley shuddered.

As Alex dragged her from the room, she spotted a man standing near the door in the distance. She recognized him as one of the local judges in the area.

She knew things were about to turn even uglier.

FORTY-SIX

"WE'VE GOT HIM."

Titus stared at Jesse as the fed tucked his phone back into his pocket. "What are you talking about?"

"Your brother. I went to a different judge and presented the evidence. He's giving me an arrest warrant. I'm going with you to find him."

His mind raced. "Don't you need to be at the rally?"

Jesse shrugged and stepped toward the door. "No, it's like I said earlier. There will be a lot of agents on-site. While they're there, I need to cut off the head of the snake, and right now that appears to be Alex. He has all the information we need."

Caution still threaded through Titus' muscles. "But he's slicker than you might think."

Jesse let out a breathy chuckle. "Oh, believe me, I

know exactly how sly he is. And if he's with Presley right now, that's where I'm going also."

"All right then. Let's go." Titus didn't want to stand around talking too much—not when every second counted.

They pulled to a stop a few houses down from Senator Gately's place. Then the two of them approached the house on foot, staying out of sight in case anyone was watching.

While Jesse went to the front of the house, Titus crept to the back door. After peering inside and seeing no one, he twisted the handle.

It was locked, of course.

Under some circumstances, he'd simply break the glass to get in. But he didn't want to announce his arrival. The element of surprise would work in his favor right now.

Instead, Titus pulled out a kit from his pocket and worked the lock until the mechanisms clicked with release.

Then he slipped inside.

As he scanned the house, he didn't see any signs of life.

He already knew that the senator and his wife weren't there. They'd been spotted in the senator's downtown office. The couple didn't have any children, so it was just the two of them living here.

"Alex's car is in the garage," Jesse said into his comm.

"Good to know," Titus muttered.

So, either his brother was here, or his brother had caught a ride with someone. But his brother was too smart to be at that rally. Where else would he have gone?

Carefully, Titus walked the perimeter inside the house.

If Alex was here, where would he be?

Did he have Presley with him? Where would he take her to get married?

Several minutes later, he and Jesse had cleared the house.

"Do you think he took her to his office?" Jesse asked.

"While she's wearing a wedding dress?" Titus frowned. "I find that hard to believe. He would take her somewhere more private." An idea hit him. "What about the pool house out back?"

"Let's go."

They both darted outside.

As soon as Titus reached it, he heard voices inside.

He was right. This was where they'd gone.

"Do you take this man to be your lawfully wedded husband?"

A cry sounded—almost like someone had been pinched and squeezed too hard.

His heart rate quickened.

If Titus was going to act, he had to act now.

As Presley stood in front of Alex, she felt beside herself. As if she wasn't living her life, but someone else's instead. Almost like she was watching something take place knowing she was powerless to stop it. Like she could speak, but her voice would never actually be heard.

Alex kept a tight grip on her hand, almost as if afraid she would run.

But she knew what would happen if she did that.

He would find her.

He might even shoot her.

Then he'd kill Titus.

Could she really do this? Could she marry Alex?

She knew she couldn't.

Ever.

Being with him had been one big mistake—one she needed to fix.

She prayed that Titus wouldn't pay the price for her choices.

"Do you take this man to be your lawfully

wedded husband?" the judge asked again as she and Alex stood before him.

Presley glanced at Alex and saw his gaze harden. She was taking too long. He needed to hurry this through.

Yet she also saw the expectation there. He fully thought he controlled her to the extent that she'd say yes.

She swallowed hard, her lungs tight as the judge waited for her response.

Her future hung in the balance right now.

She tried to loosen Alex's grip. To pull away from him.

But he held on tight.

Knowing the consequences of what she was about to do, she looked up into his gaze and refused to look away. "No. I will never be your wife, Alex Armstrong. You're a vile, evil man, and you deserve to rot in prison."

As she said the words, red-hot lava seemed to fill his gaze.

He let out a grunt, and Presley was certain if the judge wasn't here, Alex would make her pay for what she was saying.

"My love . . . there's no need for cold feet," he said. "I know this seems stressful. But I'll take good care of you. Now and forever. You have my word."

His definition of taking good care of someone was much different than hers.

Nausea turned in her gut.

He wasn't going to let her walk away, was he?

And as he stared at her, shooting daggers with his gaze, the door burst open.

"FBI! Put your hands up." One of Alex's security guards burst into the room, gun drawn, FBI badge on his pocket.

Wait . . . was this guy actually a fed?

"Alex Armstrong, you are under arrest for attempting to provide material support to a terrorist group. . . . Lower your weapon."

She looked beyond him and spotted Titus.

He was here.

And he was alive.

She nearly turned into a puddle right there.

But she couldn't. Alex still had a gun on him.

Would he be brave enough to pull it out? In front of the judge?

He stared at her a moment, his eyes narrowing, before looking back at the judge.

"This isn't over," Alex said. "These guys don't know what they're talking about. I'll be released before nightfall."

"I wouldn't be so sure about that." Jesse jerked Alex's arms behind his back and cuffed him. "And we're going to want to talk to you also, Judge. Backup is on the way."

"I'm just doing a wedding ceremony . . ." the judge muttered.

"Sure, you are." Jesse threw him a look.

Before Presley's knees completely gave out, Titus' arms surrounded her, and he pulled her into a long hug. She melted in his embrace.

"You came for me," she murmured into his chest.

He held her tight. "I'll always come for you—whenever you need me. I promise you that."

AS MUCH AS Titus wanted to stay here and hold Presley, he knew that wasn't an option. Not when so much was on the line.

Two other FBI agents had already arrived, and they would handle this scene, but the rest of his team was at the rally, and he felt certain something bad was about to happen. Alex hadn't opened up yet about what—but Jesse was going to keep working on him.

He drew back from Presley, instantly missing the warmth of her body against his. As her face came into view, he saw the mascara flooding down her cheeks. Her bloodshot eyes.

But he saw her relief. He saw the peace in her gaze.

She'd told Alex no. She'd stood up to him.

He was proud of her.

But if Titus hadn't shown up when he did, he shuddered to think about what Alex would have done to her.

"Presley, I've got to get to the rally."

"Senator Gately is involved," she blurted. "He's in on this."

"What?"

"It's true." Determination filled her gaze. "I'm going with you."

"I don't think that's a good idea." His jaw hardened when he thought about her getting hurt or being in the line of fire again. He just wanted to tuck her away somewhere safe for now—especially after spending the last few days completely worried about her.

She raised her chin. "I'm going with you. It's my choice."

He saw the stubbornness in her gaze. Presley was tired of being told what to do.

And the last thing Titus wanted was to be like his brother.

He stared at her another moment, reservations still present, before he finally nodded. "Okay then. But you don't have time to change."

"I'll be fine. Let's go."

"I'll handle the situation here," Jesse said.

Titus took Presley's hand in his. With her other hand, she hiked up her wedding dress. They hurried outside to his truck.

A moment later, they headed down the road toward the rally.

"How did you find me?" Presley rushed.

"We found a video of the taxi picking you up." Titus kept his gaze out the windshield, looking for any more signs of trouble. "Thankfully, we knew you were dropped off here."

"Alex told me he has a guy inside the FBI and that he would kill you if I didn't marry him." Presley's voice cracked, and she rubbed her throat.

His heart thumped harder—not that her words surprised him. There was very little he would put past his brother. "Alex probably does have someone on the inside. Right now, I hope the FBI truly will uncover this web of deceit."

Presley grabbed his hand, a new urgency to her voice. "We can't let them get away with this, Titus. The System is going to blame this incident on a different group. Then they'll come in and try to make the situation better, so they look like heroes. They have all these details already worked out. Alex is probably banking on getting out of jail because of this."

Titus felt his jaw harden. "That doesn't surprise

me. But that's not going to happen. Not if I have anything to do with it."

They parked as close as they could get to the rally site before climbing from the truck and darting toward the rally.

They paused on the edge of the crowd.

Thousands of people had gathered on the lawn of a city park in the center of town.

As Titus looked around, he spotted the FBI with their bomb-sniffing dogs. Security measures had definitely been stepped up.

But would that be enough?

"Titus . . ." Presley grabbed his arm and pointed to someone in the distance. "It's Duncan. He's wearing one of those police uniforms I saw."

He followed her gaze, and his eyes widened when he saw the man patrolling the area. "You're right."

Brandon strode across the lawn and joined them. "Glad you're okay, Presley. The whole team is here—even Colton and Rocco and their guys."

"Any updates?" Titus asked.

Brandon frowned as he stared at the stage in the distance. "So far, the dogs haven't found anything.

Do you think this event could be a misdirection—a smokescreen for something else?"

Presley's mind raced.

Even though she knew that could be a possibility, she didn't think it was. Not considering the fact that Alex had wanted to marry her right at this very time to give himself an alibi. *Something* was going to happen.

What were they missing?

As Brandon's phone buzzed, he glanced at it. "I got a text message from Colton. He just heard someone attempted to set off a bomb at a nearby water reservoir."

Water reservoir?

Her mind raced.

"Has that been their plan all along?" Titus frowned, and his features looked pinched with thought. "The FBI thought I'd been using my computer to research water reservoirs in the area."

Presley shook her head. "No, we're missing something. That could've been planned as a distraction. Has anyone spoken yet at this rally?"

"We've had two speakers," Brandon said. "Senator Gately is going on in ten minutes."

So, the other speakers weren't the ones Alex had been talking about.

Then what had that conversation Presley had overheard been referring to?

She scanned the crowds again, looking for some kind of sign.

As she did, her breath caught. "I know what we're missing."

The men turned to face her and waited for her explanation.

"The speaker I heard him talking about . . . it wasn't a person." She licked her lips as fear trembled through her. "It's the actual AV equipment—the speakers on the corners of the stage."

Titus' gaze darkened. "That must be where they put the bombs."

Brandon nodded toward the stage. "Let's go."

AS THE BLACKOUT team rushed to get people to safety, the crowds dispersed—in an orderly fashion, thankfully.

The System's plan had been brilliant, though.

An event like this would put Senator Gately in the spotlight. People would love him and adore him after everything he'd been through.

Then he could move in with his radical ideas and make a play.

This hadn't been a short game plan. These players were in it for the long haul. They had their entire plot worked out.

It had almost worked.

Titus just prayed they were able to get everybody out of here on time.

And what about those bombs? If Presley was right, they were on a timer.

Or was someone here simply waiting with a detonator, biding his time until he pushed a button?

Titus glanced around, wondering exactly who that would be if that was the case.

His breath caught as he recognized someone.

The leader of Dagger.

Easton Shields.

He stood next to a nearby building, leaning casually as if the crowds around him weren't scattering. His calm demeanor caused dread to pool in Titus' stomach.

Titus pressed the button on his comm. "You guys . . . Easton is here. And he looks suspicious." He told his team where to find Easton.

"Let's go get him," Brandon said.

Titus turned to Presley. "Stay here. Please."

She nodded, her eyes wide. "I will. Be safe. Titus . . . I love you."

Warmth filled his chest. "I love you too. I'll be back. I promise."

But the look in her gaze showed that she wasn't sure about that.

If the timing was just one second off . . . they could all die.

But he couldn't think like that right now.

Instead, Titus darted toward Easton.

As the man glanced up, realization spread throughout his gaze.

He took off in a run.

Before he got far, Titus tackled him on the sidewalk.

As he did, something flew from Easton's hand and skittered across the cement.

Titus' breath caught.

A detonator.

"I don't know what you think you're doing," Titus muttered.

Easton lunged for the device, his fingers only inches away.

"Oh no, you don't." Titus rose up just enough to slam Easton's arm into the ground.

As Easton struggled, someone else snatched the device.

Titus' breath caught.

Until he saw Brandon standing there.

"You won't be needing this," Brandon muttered.

The FBI surrounded them.

Titus jerked Easton to his feet and pinned his arms behind him. As he did, the FBI handcuffed him.

"You've been a part of this the whole time, haven't you? You and all your guys," Brandon muttered. "Your end goal was to bring Blackout down and eliminate your competition."

"That's why you hadn't used the detonator yet," Titus added. "You were waiting for us to get closer to the bombs."

Easton's gaze darkened. "I don't know what you're talking about."

"I think you do."

The FBI led him away as he continued to protest.

Titus felt a rush of relief. Was this really over?

Had they stopped these guys' plan?

It almost seemed too good to be true.

But he didn't think it was.

Brandon squeezed his shoulder. "Good job. You just saved thousands of people."

"We all did this," Titus said. "And I'm so glad it's over."

"We all are. Now, go find Presley."

Titus turned, his gaze going back to the area where he'd left her.

She was gone.

A moment of panic raced through him.

Then he saw her.

Walking toward him. Wearing that wedding dress. Her gaze on him.

Titus couldn't get to her fast enough. As soon as

she was close enough, he pulled her into his arms and held her tight. He never wanted to let go.

"Is it over?" she murmured into his chest.

"It is. Alex will never hurt you again. You have my word on it."

"Titus . . ." Her voice cracked with emotion as she pulled back enough to look into his gaze.

His eyes went to her lips—lips he'd been wanting to kiss ever since he'd seen her again. But she'd been off limits then.

Not anymore.

He dipped his head toward hers, and their lips met.

Titus held her tighter, not caring about the chaos around him—only about Presley.

Maybe all the bad that had happened had truly worked out for good.

EPILOGUE

TWO DAYS LATER, in Lantern Beach, Titus stood in front of Presley on the beach as the sun shone overhead. The day was glorious, the sky was blue, and the breeze refreshing.

In many ways, the weather reminded him of when he and Presley had met on a beach the first time. But unlike Virginia Beach, the shore here was empty of anyone except the people they'd invited to join them.

It seemed appropriate that Titus and Presley would be married on a beach.

Presley had donned her wedding dress—but not the one Alex had forced her to buy.

Instead, she wore a flowing white gown and flip-flops. Her hair blew in the breeze. Hardly any makeup graced her face.

She'd never looked so stunning.

Titus wore his favorite jeans with a white button-up shirt and leather sandals.

All their closest friends surrounded them—including members of Titus' team and their girlfriends. Afterwards, they would have a small reception at the Blackout headquarters, catered by a local restaurant owner named Lisa Dillinger. Even the town's police chief, Cassidy Chambers, and her husband, Ty, who cofounded Blackout, was in attendance.

The ceremony was small, but it was perfect.

Especially now that Alex was behind bars.

He along with several other members of The System were facing terrorism charges.

With Presley's help, the feds had been able to break into Alex's computer and retrieve classified documents kept under a secure server.

Presley had been able to guess the password to get in: MYLOVE.

The names of all the core members were there—including the judge, an FBI agent, a political aide, and Senator Gately.

What had happened was one of the biggest political scandals that had gone down in years. Katie Logan covered it, gaining exclusive interviews from

Blackout members. Taryn Parsons, Maddox's girl-friend, had been able to use funds left to her by Mr. Whitmore to fulfill his final wish to get answers. Finley Cooper, the CEO of Embolden Tech, had provided the necessary technology to them throughout the entire operation.

It had truly been a team effort—the team involving both official and unofficial members of Blackout.

Together, they'd been able to thwart the attack before it happened.

A sense of victory hung in the air.

Now, maybe they could all relax and enjoy this evening—at least, before any more high-stakes assignments popped up.

"Titus Armstrong, do you take this woman to be your lawfully wedded wife?" Pastor Jack Wilson asked as he stood on the shore with the ocean waves crashing behind him.

Titus felt a warmth like he'd never experienced before well up inside him as he stared at Presley. "I do."

"And Presley Lennox, do you take this man to be your lawfully wedded husband, to have and to hold from this day forward?"

Presley smiled as she gazed up at him. "I do."

"Titus Armstrong and Presley Lennox, I now pronounce you husband and wife."

At those words, Titus leaned forward and pressed his lips against hers. Not in a short kiss. But in a kiss he'd dreamed about for years.

Applause sounded around him as their friends stood and surrounded them.

Titus flashed Presley a smile as he leaned back.

Then he turned to his friends. "You're all next to tie the knot. My bets are on Brandon, but any of you really are a possibility."

Brandon grinned at Finley Cooper, his girlfriend, and winked. "We might be able to make that happen. But only if Maddox agrees to crochet my tuxedo jacket and Dylan reads poetry."

"I'll get started on that now," Maddox said as he slipped his arm around Taryn.

Another round of chuckles followed.

Maybe—just maybe—for today, the world was a better, safer place.

At least, Titus knew that the world was a happier place—for him.

Because he had Presley by his side.

~~~
~~~

Thank you for reading *Titus*. If you enjoyed this book, please consider leaving a review!

If you liked getting to know Jesse Marx, stayed tuned for *Forgotten Secrets*, the first book in the Vanishing Ranch series, featuring none other than . . . Jesse Marx! You can preorder your copy HERE.

ALSO BY CHRISTY BARRITT:

OTHER BOOKS IN THE LANTERN BEACH SERIES:

LANTERN BEACH MYSTERIES

Hidden Currents

You can take the detective out of the investigation, but you can't take the investigator out of the detective. A notorious gang puts a bounty on Detective Cady Matthews's head after she takes down their leader, leaving her no choice but to hide until she can testify at trial. But her temporary home across the country on a remote North Carolina island isn't as peaceful as she initially thinks. Living under the new identity of Cassidy Livingston, she struggles to keep her investigative skills tucked away, especially after a body washes ashore. When local police bungle the murder investigation, she can't resist stepping in. But Cassidy is supposed to be keeping a low profile. One wrong move could lead to both her discovery and her demise. Can she bring justice to the island . . . or will the hidden currents surrounding her pull her under for good?

Flood Watch

The tide is high, and so is the danger on Lantern Beach. Still in hiding after infiltrating a dangerous gang, Cassidy Livingston just has to make it a few more months before she can testify at trial and resume her old life. But trouble keeps finding her, and Cassidy is pulled into a local investigation after a man mysteriously disappears from the island she now calls home. A recurring nightmare from her time undercover only muddies things, as does a visit from the parents of her handsome ex-Navy SEAL neighbor. When a friend's life is threatened, Cassidy must make choices that put her on the verge of blowing her cover. With a flood watch on her emotions and her life in a tangle, will Cassidy find the truth? Or will her past finally drown her?

Storm Surge

A storm is brewing hundreds of miles away, but its effects are devastating even from afar. Laid-back, loose, and light: that's Cassidy Livingston's new motto. But when a makeshift boat with a bloody cloth inside washes ashore near her oceanfront home, her detective instincts shift into gear . . . again. Seeking clues isn't the only thing on her mind—romance is heating up with next-door neighbor and former Navy SEAL Ty Chambers as well. Her heart wants the love and stability she's longed for her entire life. But her hidden identity only leads to a tidal wave of turbulence. As more answers emerge about the boat, the danger around her rises, creating a treacherous swell that threatens to reveal her past. Can Cassidy mind her own business, or will the storm surge of violence and corruption that has washed ashore on Lantern Beach leave her life in wreckage?

Dangerous Waters

Danger lurks on the horizon, leaving only two choices: find shelter or flee. Cassidy Livingston's new identity has begun to feel as comfortable as her favorite sweater. She's been tucked away on Lantern Beach for weeks, waiting to testify against a deadly gang, and is settling in to a new life she wants to last forever. When she thinks she spots someone malevolent from her past, panic swells inside her. If an enemy has found her, Cassidy won't be the only one who's a target. Everyone she's come to love will also be at risk. Dangerous waters threaten to pull her into an overpowering chasm she may never escape. Can

Cassidy survive what lies ahead? Or has the tide fatally turned against her?

Perilous Riptide

Just when the current seems safer, an unseen danger emerges and threatens to destroy everything. When Cassidy Livingston finds a journal hidden deep in the recesses of her ice cream truck, her curiosity kicks into high gear. Islanders suspect that Elsa, the journal's owner, didn't die accidentally. Her final entry indicates their suspicions might be correct and that what Elsa observed on her final night may have led to her demise. Against the advice of Ty Chambers, her former Navy SEAL boyfriend, Cassidy taps into her detective skills and hunts for answers. But her search only leads to a skeletal body and trouble for both of them. As helplessness threatens to drown her, Cassidy is desperate to turn back time. Can Cassidy find what she needs to navigate the perilous situation? Or will the riptide surrounding her threaten everyone and everything Cassidy loves?

Deadly Undertow

The current's fatal pull is powerful, but so is one detective's will to live. When someone from Cassidy Livingston's past shows up on Lantern Beach and warns her of impending peril, opposing currents collide, threatening to drag her under. Running would be easy. But leaving would break her heart. Cassidy must decipher between the truth and lies, between reality and deception. Even more importantly, she must decide whom to trust and whom to fear. Her life depends on it. As danger rises and answers surface, everything Cassidy thought she knew is tested. In order to survive, Cassidy must take drastic measures and end the battle against the ruthless gang DH-7 once and for all. But if her final mission fails, the consequences will be as deadly as the raging undertow.

LANTERN BEACH ROMANTIC SUSPENSE

Tides of Deception

Change has come to Lantern Beach: a new police chief, a new season, and . . . a new romance? Austin Brooks has loved Skye Lavinia from the moment they met, but the walls she keeps around her seem impenetrable. Skye knows Austin is the best thing to ever happen to her. Yet she also knows that if he learns the truth about her past, he'd be a fool not to run. A chance encounter brings secrets bubbling to the surface, and danger soon follows. Are the life-threatening events plaguing them really accidents . . . or is someone trying to send a deadly message? With the tides on Lantern Beach come deception and lies. One question remains—who will be swept away as the water shifts? And will it bring the end for Austin and Skye, or merely the beginning?

Shadow of Intrigue

For her entire life, Lisa Garth has felt like a supporting character in the drama of life. The designation never bothered her—until now. Lantern Beach, where she's settled and runs a popular restaurant, has boarded up for the season. The slower pace leaves her with too much time alone. Braden Dillinger came to Lantern Beach to try to heal. The former Special Forces officer returned from battle with invisible scars and diminished hope. But his recovery is hampered by the fact that an unknown enemy is trying to kill him. From the moment Lisa and Braden meet, danger ignites around them, and both are drawn into a web of intrigue that turns their lives upside down. As shadows creep in, will Lisa and Braden be able to shine a light on the peril around them? Or will the encroaching darkness turn their worst nightmares into reality?

Storm of Doubt

A pastor who's lost faith in God. A romance

writer who's lost faith in love. A faceless man with a deadly obsession. Nothing has felt right in Pastor Jack Wilson's world since his wife died two years ago. He hoped coming to Lantern Beach might help soothe the ragged edges of his soul. Instead, he feels more alone than ever. Novelist Juliette Grace came to the island to hide away. Though her professional life has never been better, her personal life has imploded. Her husband left her and a stalker's threats have grown more and more dangerous. When Jack saves Juliette from an attack, he sees the terror in her gaze and knows he must protect her. But when danger strikes again, will Jack be able to keep her safe? Or will the approaching storm prove too strong to withstand?

Winds of Danger

Wes O'Neill is perfectly content to hang with his friends and enjoy island life on Lantern Beach. Something begins to change inside him when Paige Henderson sweeps into his life. But the beautiful newcomer is hiding painful secrets beneath her cheerful facade. Police dispatcher Paige Henderson came to Lantern Beach riddled with guilt and uncertainties after the fallout of a bad relationship. When she meets Wes, she begins to open up to the possibility of love again. But there's something Wes isn't telling her—something that could change everything. As the winds shift, doubts seep into Paige's mind. Can Paige and Wes trust each other, even as the currents work against them? Or is trouble from the past too much to overcome?

Rains of Remorse

A stranger invades her home, leaving Rebecca Jarvis terrified. Above all, she must protect the baby growing inside her. Since her estranged husband died suspiciously six months earlier, Rebecca has been determined to depend on no one but herself. Her chivalrous new neighbor appears to be an answer to prayer. But who is Levi Stoneman really? Rebecca wants to believe he can help her, but she can't ignore her instincts. As danger closes in, both Rebecca and Levi must figure out whom they can trust. With Rebecca's baby coming soon, there's no time to waste. Can the truth prevail . . . or will remorse overpower the best of intentions?

Torrents of Fear

The woman lingering in the crowd can't be Allison . . . can she? Because Allison was pronounced dead six years ago. Musician Carter Denver knows only one person who's capable of helping him find answers: Sadie Thompson, his estranged best friend and someone who also knew Allison. He needs to know if he's losing his mind or if Allison could have survived her car accident. Could Allison really be alive? If so, why is she trying to harm Carter and Sadie? As the two try to find answers, can Sadie keep her feelings for Carter hidden? Could he ever care for her, or is the man of her dreams still in love with the woman now causing his nightmares?

LANTERN BEACH PD

On the Lookout

When Cassidy Chambers accepted the job as police chief on Lantern Beach, she knew the island had its secrets. But a suspicious death with potentially far-reaching implications will test all her skills —and threaten to reveal her true identity. Cassidy enlists the help of her husband, former Navy SEAL Ty Chambers. As they dig for answers, both uncover parts of their pasts that are best left buried. Not everything is as it seems, and they must figure out if their John Doe is connected to the secretive group that has moved onto the island. As facts materialize, danger on the island grows. Can Cassidy and Ty discover the truth about the shadowy crimes in their cozy community? Or has darkness permanently invaded their beloved Lantern Beach?

Attempt to Locate

A fun girls' night out turns into a nightmare when armed robbers barge into the store where Cassidy and her friends are shopping. As the situation escalates and the men escape, a massive manhunt launches on Lantern Beach to apprehend the dangerous trio. In the midst of the chaos, a potential foe asks for Cassidy's help. He needs to find his sister who fled from the secretive Gilead's Cove community on the island. But the more Cassidy learns about the seemingly untouchable group, the more her unease grows. The pressure to solve both cases continues to mount. But as the gravity of the situation rises, so does the danger. Cassidy is determined to protect the island and break up the cult . . . but doing so might cost her everything.

First Degree Murder

Police Chief Cassidy Chambers longs for a break from the recent crimes plaguing Lantern Beach. She simply wants to enjoy her friends' upcoming wedding, to prepare for the busy tourist season about to slam the island, and to gather all the dirt she can on the suspicious community that's invaded the town. But trouble explodes on the island, sending residents—including Cassidy—into a squall of uneasiness. Cassidy may have more than one enemy plotting her demise, and the collateral damage seems unthinkable. As the temperature rises, so does the pressure to find answers. Someone is determined that Lantern Beach would be better off without their new police chief. And for Cassidy, one wrong move could mean certain death.

Dead on Arrival

With a highly charged local election consuming the community, Police Chief Cassidy Chambers braces herself for a challenging day of breaking up petty conflicts and tamping down high emotions. But when widespread food poisoning spreads among potential voters across the island, Cassidy smells something rotten in the air. As Cassidy examines every possibility to uncover what's going on, local enigma Anthony Gilead again comes on her radar. The man is running for mayor and his cult-like following is growing at an alarming rate. Cassidy feels certain he has a spy embedded in her inner circle. The problem is that her pool of suspects gets deeper every day. Can Cassidy get to the bottom of what's eating away at her peaceful island home? Will voters turn out despite the outbreak of illness plaguing their tranquil town? And the even bigger question: Has darkness come to stay on Lantern Beach?

Plan of Action

A missing Navy SEAL. Danger at the boiling point. The ultimate showdown. When Police Chief Cassidy Chambers' husband, Ty, disappears, her world is turned upside down. His truck is discovered with blood inside, crashed in a ditch on Lantern Beach, but he's nowhere to be found. As they launch a manhunt to find him, Cassidy discovers that someone on the island has a deadly obsession with Ty. Meanwhile, Gilead's Cove seems to be imploding. As danger heightens, federal law enforcement officials are called in. The cult's growing threat could lead to the pinnacle standoff of good versus evil. A clear plan of action is needed or the results will be devastating. Will Cassidy find Ty in time, or will she face a gut-wrenching loss? Will Anthony Gilead finally be unmasked for who he really is and be brought to justice? Hundreds of innocent lives are at stake . . . and not everyone will come out alive.

LANTERN BEACH BLACKOUT

Dark Water

Colton Locke can't forget the black op that went terribly wrong. Desperate for a new start, he moves to Lantern Beach, North Carolina, and forms Blackout, a private security firm. Despite his hero status, he can't erase the mistakes he's made. For the past year, Elise Oliver hasn't been able to shake the feeling that there's more to her husband's death than she was told. When she finds a hidden box of his personal possessions, more questions—and suspicions—arise. The only person she trusts to help her is her husband's best friend, Colton Locke. Someone wants Elise dead. Is it because she knows too much? Or is it to keep her from finding the truth? The Blackout team must uncover dark secrets hiding beneath seemingly still waters. But those very secrets might just tear the team apart.

Safe Harbor

Guilt over past mistakes haunts former Navy SEAL Dez Rodriguez. When he's asked to guard a pop star during a music festival on Lantern Beach, he's all set for what he hopes is a breezy assignment. Bree hasn't found fame to be nearly as fulfilling as she dreamed. Instead, she's more like a carefully crafted character living out a pre-scripted story. When a stalker's threats become deadly, her life—and career—are turned upside down. From the start, Bree sees her temporary bodyguard as a player, and Dez sees Bree as a spoiled rich girl. But when they're thrown together in a fight for survival, both must learn to trust. Can Dez protect Bree—and his carefully guarded heart? Or will their safe harbor ultimately become their death trap?

Ripple Effect

Griff McIntyre never expected his ex-wife and three-year-old daughter to come to Lantern Beach. After an abduction attempt, they're desperate for safety. Now Griff's not letting either of them out of his sight. Bethany knows Griff is the only one who can protect them, despite the fact that he broke her heart. But she'll do anything to keep her daughter safe—even if it means playing nicely with a man she can't stand. As peril ripples through their lives, Griff and Bethany must work together to protect their daughter. But an unseen enemy wants something from them . . . and will stop at nothing to get it. When disaster strikes, can Griff keep his family safe? Or will past mistakes bring the ultimate failure?

Rising Tide

Benjamin James knows there's a traitor within his former command. The rest of his team might even think it's him. As danger closes in, he must clear himself and stop a deadly plot by a dangerous terrorist group. All CJ Compton wanted was a new start after her career ended under suspicion. Working as the house manager for private security group

Blackout seems perfect. But there's more trouble here than what she left behind. As the tide rushes in, the stakes continue to rise. If the Blackout team fails, it's not just Lantern Beach at stake—it's the whole country. Can Benjamin and CJ overcome their differences and work together to find the truth?

LANTERN BEACH BLACKOUT: THE NEW RECRUITS

Rocco

Former Navy SEAL and new Blackout recruit Rocco Foster is on a simple in and out mission. But the operation turns complicated when an unsuspecting woman wanders into the line of fire. Peyton Ellison's life mission is to sprinkle happiness on those around her. When a cupcake delivery turns into a fight for survival, she must trust her rescuer—a handsome stranger—to keep her safe. Rocco is determined to figure out why someone is targeting Peyton. First, he must keep the intriguing woman safe and earn her trust. But threats continue to pummel them as incriminating evidence emerges and pits them against each other. With time running out, the two must set aside both their growing attraction and their doubts about each other in order to work together. But the perilous facts they discover leave them wondering what exactly the truth is . . . and if the truth can be trusted.

Axel

Women are missing. Private security firm Blackout must find them before another victim disappears. Axel Hendrix likes to live on the edge. That's why being a Navy SEAL suited him so well. But after his last mission, he cut his losses and joined Blackout instead. His team's latest case involves an undercover investigation on Lantern Beach. Olivia Rollins came to the island to escape her problems—and danger. When trouble from her past shows up in town, she impulsively blurts she's engaged to Axel, the womanizing man she's seen while waitressing. Now, she may not be the only one in danger. So could Axel. Axel knows Olivia might be his chance to find answers and that acting like her fiancé is the perfect cover for his latest assignment. But he doesn't like throwing Olivia into the middle of such a dangerous situation. Nor is he comfortable with the feelings she stirs inside him. With Olivia's life—as well as both their hearts—on the line, Axel must uncover the truth and stop an evil plan before more lives are destroyed.

Beckett

When the daughter of a federal judge is abducted, private security firm Blackout must find her. Psychologist Samantha Reynolds doesn't know why someone is targeting her. Even after a risky mission to save her, danger still lingers. She's determined to use her insights into the human mind to help decode the deadly clues being left in the wake of her rescue. Former Navy SEAL Beckett Jones needs to figure out who's responsible for the crimes hounding Sami. He's not sure why he's so protective of the woman he rescued, but he'll do anything to keep her safe—even if it means risking his heart. As the body count rises, there's no room for error. Beckett and Sami must both tear down the careful walls they've built around themselves in order to survive. If they don't figure out who's responsible, the madman will continue his death spree . . . and one of them might be next.

Gabe

When former Navy SEAL and current Blackout operative Gabe Michaels is almost killed in a hit-and-run, the aftermath completely upends his life. He's no longer safe—and he's not the only one. Dr. Autumn Spenser came to Lantern Beach to start fresh. But while treating Gabe after his accident, she senses there's more to what happened to him than meets the eye. When she digs deeper into his past, she never expects to be drawn into a deadly dilemma. Gabe has been infatuated with the pretty doctor since the day they met. Now, can he keep her from harm? Could someone out of his league ever return his feelings or will her past hurts keep them apart? As danger continues to pummel them, Gabe and Autumn are thrown together in a quest to find answers. More important than their growing attraction, they must stay alive long enough to stop the person desperate to destroy them.

LANTERN BEACH BLACKOUT: DANGER RISING

Brandon

Physically he's protecting her. But emotionally she's never felt more exposed. The last person tech heiress Finley Cooper ever wanted to see again was Brandon Hale. Two years ago, Brandon shattered her heart. Now Finley needs protection, and, against her wishes, Brandon is assigned the job. Even worse, they must pretend to be a couple in order to find answers. Brandon, a former Navy SEAL, met Finley while on an undercover assignment in Ecuador. But he broke her trust, and now he doesn't blame Finley for hating him. As a new Blackout operative, Brandon's first assignment throws him into Finley's life 24/7. Someone wants her dead, and it's clear this person won't stop until that mission is accomplished. To keep her safe, Brandon must regain Finley's trust. Can he convince her she's more than a job to him? Or will peril permanently silence them?

Dylan

His job is to protect her. The trouble is . . . she doesn't want protection. Former Navy SEAL Dylan Granger's new assignment requires him to use both his tactical abilities and his acting skills. Hired by Katie Logan's father, his job is to protect the gutsy university professor while concealing his identity. To maintain his cover, he takes the unassuming role of her new assistant. Katie—a disgraced reporter—has stumbled upon a lead she can't ignore. Now it's clear someone is targeting her, but she refuses to back down. Her handsome new assistant is a welcome distraction from the chaos. But Dylan's skillset goes way beyond his job description, and Katie begins to suspect there's more to Dylan than he's letting on. Dylan's mission can't be disclosed—not if he wants to keep Katie safe. But as his feelings for her grow and the danger increases, keeping his secret becomes more of a challenge than he ever imagined. With innocent lives on the line, Dylan must choose between protecting Katie or savings others.

Run Aground

A dead captain on a luxury yacht leads to a tumultuous seafaring journey . . . Med student Kenzie Anderson, tired of letting others chart her future, accepts a job as second steward aboard *Almost Paradise*. But when she finds the captain dead before the charter even begins, her plans seem to capsize. Jimmy James Gamble senses something vulnerable and slightly naive about Kenzie when he finds her on the docks. Realizing danger may still be lingering close, he uses his hidden skills to earn a place on the charter. But being there causes him to risk everything —especially as more suspicious incidents occur. As they set out to sea, Kenzie and Jimmy James both wonder if they're in over their heads. They must figure out how to stop a killer before anyone onboard is hurt . . . otherwise, both their futures might just run aground.

Dead Reckoning

A yachtie fears for her life when she's the only witness to a murder . . . Kenzie Anderson knows what she saw at the harbor—a woman strangled and pushed overboard. But there's no proof of a crime . . . only her word. Jimmy James Gamble believes Kenzie, even if no one else does. As he senses the danger in the air, all he wants is to keep her away from any more trouble—especially after their last charter. Either Kenzie or the yacht they're working on seem to be a magnet for murder and mayhem. Someone is willing to kill to get what he wants—and will do so again if necessary. Can Jimmy James and Kenzie navigate these unfamiliar waters? Or will relying on dead reckoning lead them to their deaths?

Tipping Point

Awakening in a boat surrounded by nothing but water, a yachtie has no doubt someone wants her dead. Kenzie Anderson is determined not to let anyone scare her away from completing the charter season—even with the threats on her life. The only person she can trust is Captain Jimmy James Gamble, despite their tumultuous relationship. Kenzie and Jimmy James both suspect turbulent currents rush beneath the tranquil surface aboard the luxury yacht *Almost Paradise*. Secrets seem to abound, each one increasing the tension aboard the boat. As answers rise to the surface, neither Kenzie nor Jimmy James is prepared for what they find. Have they both reached their tipping points? Their adversaries want nothing more than to make Kenzie disappear . . . forever. It may be too late for a mayday call.

ABOUT THE AUTHOR

USA Today has called Christy Barritt's books "scary, funny, passionate, and quirky."

Christy writes both mystery and romantic suspense novels that are clean with underlying messages of faith. Her books have won the Daphne du Maurier Award for Excellence in Suspense and Mystery, have been twice nominated for the Romantic Times Reviewers' Choice Award, and have finaled for both a Carol Award and Foreword Magazine's Book of the Year.

She is married to her Prince Charming, a man who thinks she's hilarious—but only when she's not trying to be. Christy is a self-proclaimed klutz, an avid music lover who's known for spontaneously bursting into song, and a road trip aficionado.

When she's not working or spending time with her family, she enjoys singing, playing the guitar, and exploring small, unsuspecting towns where people have no idea how accident-prone she is.

Find Christy online at:
www.christybarritt.com
www.facebook.com/christybarritt
www.twitter.com/cbarritt

Sign up for Christy's newsletter to get information on all of her latest releases here: **www.christybarritt. com/newsletter-sign-up/**

www.ingramcontent.com/pod-product-compliance
Lightning Source LLC
Chambersburg PA
CBHW031955150726
47990CB00005B/1724